Les Misérables

Children's Edition

By Victor Hugo

Abridged and Edited by Matt Larsen

2018

Also abridged by Matt Larsen:

Les Misérables: High School Edition

Les Misérables: Ultimate Fan Edition

Written by Matt Larsen:

Benjamin Rush: Revolutionary Relationships

ISBN: 9781973545699

For: Emma,
Jacob,
Spencer,
and Amelia

TABLE OF CONTENTS

Prologue

So long as there are laws that condemn the poor; society that allows poverty, starvation, and the abuse of children; so long as we ignore these problems and allow misery to remain on earth; books like this cannot be useless.

PART ONE: FANTINE

CHAPTER 1: THE BISHOP

In 1815, Charles Bienvenu Myriel was the Bishop of Digne. The Bishop's home was like a palace; spacious and beautiful. It was built of stone and had an air of greatness about it. There was the iBishop's room, the court of honor, the side chambers, all very large with arched walkways between them. There was a garden planted with magnificent trees, and the dining hall was a long superb gallery which opened into the garden.

Next door was the hospital; a low, narrow, one story building with a small garden.

One day when the Bishop had finished visiting the sick in the hospital, he invited the director of the hospital to come with him into his palace.

"Director, how many patients do you have?" inquired the Bishop.

"Twenty-six beds," said the director. "They are very crowded, and the ventilation is poor, but at least we have clean sheets. Alas, when a sickness strikes the whole town we sometimes have more than one hundred patients and we have no room for them. But what can we do, bishop? This is all we have."

They continued talking until they entered the bishop's dining hall and suddenly the bishop stopped and was silent. He turned towards the director and said:

"How many beds do you think this hall alone

would contain?"

"Your dining hall?" exclaimed the director, confused.

The bishop ran his eyes over the hall, measuring it in his head and making calculations.

It will hold twenty beds, he thought to himself.

"Director" said the bishop, "There is obviously a mistake here. There are twenty-six of you in a tiny hospital, and only three of us in this whole palace. We have room for sixty at least with all our rooms. We must fix this mistake. You may have my house and I will have yours. Here is the key; this palace is now your hospital."

The next day, all twenty-six patients were moved into the bishop's palace, and the bishop and his two sisters moved into the hospital.

When the people of the town heard of the bishop's generosity, they began donating large sums of money to the church. People knocked on the bishop's door all day and all night; some to give, and some to receive. He never kept any money for himself; never bought himself nice things, and he was so welcoming of the poor that the townspeople called him by his middle name *Bienvenu,* which means "Welcome."

The bishop's new home only had six rooms: the dining room, the prayer room, his bedroom with a guest room attached, and one room for each of his sisters.

Nothing could be plainer than the bishop's new

home: a window, a bookcase, a fireplace that seldom held a fire and a cross hanging above the mantle. There was a large table with an inkstand where the Bishop wrote his sermons, and a dining table with two vases of flowers resting upon it.

The bishop had only kept one bit of luxury: his silver. There were six silver dishes with a silver soup ladle, and two massive silver candlesticks.

Not a door in the house had a lock. At night, the door was closed only with a latch. At any hour, anyone walking by could open the door with a simple push. At first this had made his sisters very nervous. The bishop had said to them: "have bolts on your bedroom doors, if you like." Eventually they shared his confidence, and all three lived with no locks on their doors. When one sister would worry he would point at two lines written by him on the margin of a Bible: "The door of a physician should never be closed; the door of a priest should always be open."

A visitor once asked him if he did not fear that something bad would happen since his house had no locks. Bishop Bienvenu simply replied: "Unless God protects a house, they who guard it, watch in vain."

CHAPTER 2: JEAN VALJEAN

Jean Valjean was born to a poor peasant family in Faverolles. He lost his parents when he was very young. His mother died of a fever: his father, a pruner before him, was killed when he fell from the top of a tree. Jean Valjean had but one relative left, his sister, who was a widow with seven children. Valjean was forced at a young age to become the provider for his sister's family. He worked all day, leaving no time to find a wife or make a family of his own. He earned eighteen cents per day as a pruner in the summers and he worked during the winter doing whatever he could find.

That second winter caring for his sister's family was bitter cold. Valjean couldn't find work, and the family had no bread for seven starving children.

One Sunday night, the local baker was just going to bed when he heard a violent crash below in his bakery. He ran downstairs in time to see an arm reaching through the broken window and grabbing a loaf of bread. The baker ran as fast as he could down the stairs and out the door to catch the thief. When he ran him down, he found that the thief was Jean Valjean.

Valjean was convicted and sentenced to five years in the prison at Toulon. He arrived at the prison on a cart, with a chain around his neck, dressed in red, and was told he no longer had a name. Prisoners didn't deserve names. He was now to be called by a number: 24601.

Four years he spent working in prison, building enormous strength till he was the strongest of all the prisoners. He was so strong he could have lifted a car all by himself, and was nicknamed "Jean the Jack." His fellow prisoners convinced him that instead of waiting an entire fifth year to be released, he should use his strength to escape early. He climbed the prison wall by wedging himself in the corner and using his immense strength to get up and over the top of the wall.

Two days later he was caught and sentenced to an additional three years in prison. Jean didn't learn. He tried to escape again in his sixth year, then again in his tenth, and he even made a fourth escape attempt in his thirteenth year. Each time the court added more years to his sentence, until finally he served a total of nineteen years.

He had entered the prison a young man who had tried to help starving children. He left prison an old, angry, and vengeful convict.

In nineteen years he had earned a hundred and nine dollars and fifteen cents through prison labor. He was given this money along with a yellow passport, and sent out the door. The year was 1815.

He walked all day in the dust and the heat. About an hour before sunset he entered the little town of Digne. It would have been hard to find a traveler with a more wretched appearance. A slouched leather cap half hid his sun bronzed face which was dripping with sweat. His shaggy chest was visible through his torn red shirt.

He walked with weary step into the mayor's office and then came out headed for the inn. He could smell the goose roasting on the spit; could see the saucepans full of boiling stew. He practically collapsed into a seat as the Innkeeper asked "What will you have?"

"Something to eat and a place to sleep."

"Nothing could be easier" said the innkeeper, who then looked at the traveler more closely and added "for pay."

Valjean drew from his pocket a large leather purse, and answered "I have money."

"Then," said the innkeeper, "I am at your service."

Just then a policeman arrived from City hall and whispered something in the Innkeeper's ear.

"Is dinner ready?" Valjean asked.

"Sir, I cannot feed you dinner, I have no food to spare."

"What do you mean? I'm happy to pay for it."

"It's not a question of money. I also cannot lodge you here, there is no room in my Inn."

"Well put me in the stable then."

"I cannot, the horses take all the room"

"Well" said Valjean, "then I'll sleep in the corner on a pile of straw, but we'll see to that after dinner."

"I cannot feed you, all the food is reserved for

those men over there."

Valjean nearly choked as he said "There are only twelve of them. You have enough food for twenty! I am dying with hunger. I have walked since sunrise; I will pay, and I want something to eat!"

"Get Out!" said the Innkeeper. Then he leaned in close and whispered "I know who you are. Your name is Jean Valjean. I know what you've done. Now go away convict."

Valjean bowed his head, picked up his knapsack, and went out. He went to the inn three streets over. It took less than five minutes for the inn keeper to grab Valjean by the shoulder and say "clear out of here."

He was turned away at every inn in town. He began knocking on the doors of random houses, but everyone turned him away. He even crawled into a dog house, but the dog bit him and chased him off.

Exhausted, with no hope of a bed or even a pile of straw, Valjean finally lay down on a stone bench and tried to sleep.

"What are you doing there, my friend?" said a woman passing by.

He replied harshly and with anger in his voice: "I am going to sleep."

"On the bench?" she asked.

"For nineteen years I have had a wooden mattress, tonight I have a stone one."

"Why don't you go to the inn?"

"They turned me away. I have knocked at every door. Everybody has driven me away." He said gruffly.

The woman touched the man's arm and pointed to a little low house beside a large hospital.

"Have you knocked at that door there?"

"No."

"Knock there."

CHAPTER 3: THE WORTH OF SILVER

The Bishop of Digne sat writing his sermon while his sisters talked about the gossip in town. A suspicious vagabond, a convict, was lurking somewhere in the town. He might attack anyone at any time. The police had told everyone to lock, bolt, and bar their doors for safety from this vagrant.

One of the sisters turned to Bishop Bienvenu and said:

"Brother, this house is not safe at all; let me go get the locksmith to put bolts on our door. It will take but a minute. Right now, we are in great danger, not to mention the fact that you have a terrible habit of always saying 'Come in,' even at midnight! You never bother to see who it is or what they want, you just say-"

At this moment there was a violent knock on the door.

"Come in!" said the bishop.

The door opened quickly as if pushed by someone with great strength.

A man stepped through the door way with a knapsack on his back, a stick in his hand, and a fierce look in his eyes. Without waiting for the bishop to speak, the man said in a loud voice: "See here! My name is Jean Valjean. I am a convict; I have been nineteen years in prison. I have walked all day and when I reached this place I went to an inn, and they sent me away on account of my yellow passport. I went to another inn; they said: 'Get out!' Nobody would have me. Finally, a good woman showed me your house, and said: 'Knock there!' I have knocked. What is this place? Are you an inn? I am starving with hunger. Can I stay? I will pay."

"Sister," said the bishop, "put on another plate."

Valjean stepped into the light of the room. "Stop," he exclaimed. "Did you understand me? I am a galley-slave, a convict." He drew from his pocket a large sheet of yellow paper. "Here is my passport, yellow as you see. It says 'this man is very dangerous.'

The bishop looked the man straight in the eye and said warmly:

"Sir, sit down and warm yourself, dinner is ready, and your bed will be prepared while you eat."

Valjean began to stutter with surprise.

"You won't send me away? But I'm a convict!" Valjean stuttered in surprise: "You even called me Sir! I shall have a supper? A bed like other people with mattress and sheets- a real bed! It's been nineteen years since I have slept on a bed. You are good people!"

"Sister," said the bishop, "put his plate as near the fire as you can." Then turning towards his guest, he added: "You must be cold from the wind, good Sir."

Every time the Bishop said the word 'Sir,' Valjean's face lit up.

"Sir Bishop," said the man, "you are a good man. You take me into your house; you make me dinner, and you don't care who I am or where I came from."

The bishop touched his hand gently and said: "You need not tell me who you are. This is not my house; it is the house of Christ. It does not ask any comer whether he has a name, but whether he has any pain. You are suffering; you are hungry and thirsty. You don't need to tell me your name. Besides, before you told me, I knew it."

Valjean looked at the bishop, confused:

"Really? You knew my name?"

"Yes," answered the bishop, "your name is, 'my brother'."

Valjean stared at him in shocked silence.

Dinner was ready. The bishop said the blessing, and then served the soup himself with the silver ladle. Valjean ate ravenously from a silver bowl like a starving beast. The bishop moved one of the silver candlesticks closer to Valjean to help him see, and then filled his bowl again with another ladle full of soup.

As dinner ended Bishop Bienvenu took one of the lighted silver candlesticks from the table, handed the other to his guest, and led Valjean into the spare room with a clean white bed.

"Come," said the bishop, "a good night's rest to you: tomorrow morning, before you go, you shall have a cup of warm milk from our cows."

The Bishop offered a short prayer, and walked back into his own bedroom.

Valjean was so completely exhausted that he did

not even crawl between the clean white sheets; he blew out the candle with a snort of his nose, after the manner of convicts, and fell on the bed, fully dressed, and instantly fell sound sleep.

As the cathedral clock struck two, Jean Valjean awoke.

What awoke him was too good a bed. For nearly twenty years he had not slept in a bed, and the soft comfort of a real mattress was too foreign for his body to accept.

He opened his eyes, and looked around in the darkness. He listened. Not a sound.

He got up and started walking toward the door, carefully avoiding the furniture. He could hear the calm, quiet breathing of the sleeping bishop.

Valjean went quickly to the cupboard in the dining room. He opened it, took the silver dishes and ladle, crossed the room with hasty stride and put the silver in his knapsack. Then he ran out the back door, crossed the garden, leaped over the wall like a tiger, and fled.

The next day at sunrise, Bishop Bienvenu was walking in the garden when he heard his sister screaming "Sir, Sir! The silver is gone, good heavens! It is stolen. That man who came last night took it."

The bishop was silent for a moment, then raising his serious eyes, he said mildly to his sister:

"Did the silver really belong to us? It belonged to the poor. Who was this man? A poor man apparently."

"But Sir, what are going to eat with now?"

"I guess we'll use wooden plates," he said as he walked back into the house.

Just then there was a knock at the door.

"Come in," said the bishop like always.

The door opened. Three men were holding a fourth by the collar. The three men were policemen; the fourth was Jean Valjean.

The police chief advanced towards the bishop, giving a military salute. "Sir," he said.

"Ah, there you are!" said the bishop, interrupting the policeman and looking towards Jean Valjean, "I am glad to see you. But! I gave you the candlesticks also, which are silver like the rest and are worth at least two hundred dollars. Why did you not take them along with the rest?"

Jean Valjean opened his eyes and looked at the bishop dumbfounded.

"Sir," said the police chief, "then what this man said was true? He was running away with this silver so we arrested him-"

"And he told you," interrupted the bishop again with a smile, "that it had been given him by a good old priest with whom he had passed the night."

"Yes. Yes, he did say that," said the police chief confused. "So, we can let him go?"

"Certainly," replied the bishop. "Thank you for your service officers, you may go."

As the officers walked out the door the bishop went to the fireplace, took the two silver candlesticks and brought them to Jean Valjean.

The bishop said in a low voice: "Never forget what has happened here. You must promise me to use this silver to become an honest man. Jean Valjean, my brother: you belong no longer to evil, but to good. It is your soul that I am buying for you. I withdraw it from dark thoughts and from the spirit of evil and I give it to God!"

Chapter 4: Little Gervais

Jean Valjean ran from the city as if he were trying to escape. What had just happened to him? What did it mean?

While lost in his thoughts a little boy came skipping down the path toward him. The boy was singing and tossing some coins in the air. As the boy passed Jean Valjean, he tossed the coins once again but one of them fell from his hands and rolled near Valjean's foot.

Jean Valjean moved his foot on top of it.

The boy had followed the coin with his eye, and looked up at Valjean.

"Sir, my coin if you please?"

"What is your name?" said Jean Valjean.

"Little Gervais, Sir."

"Get out of here," growled Jean Valjean.

"Sir," continued the boy, "give me my coin."

Jean Valjean dropped his head and did not answer.

The child begged again:

"My coin, Sir! Give me my coin!"

The boy bent down and pushed at Valjean's heavy shoe.

"I want my coin! My fifty-cent piece!"

The child began to cry. "Move your foot, please! Please!"

Jean Valjean looked at him with a wild ferocious

look of anger and raised his fist.

"You'd better clear out little boy!"

The boy looked at him in terror, then began to tremble from head to toe and ran away as fast as he could.

Jean Valjean stood there staring at the ground. He didn't know who he was. Was he the convict he had become over two decades in prison, or was he the bishop's brother? Had his soul really been bought for God? Who was he? What version of himself would he choose?

Valjean moved his foot, bent down, and picked up the coin. He looked around, straining his eyes to see as far as possible in all directions.

He saw nothing. Night was falling; the countryside was cold and bare.

He began to run in the direction the child had gone calling out: "Little Gervais! Little Gervais!"

He listened. There was no answer.

He began to run faster and called out in a desolate and terrified voice:

"Little Gervais! Little Gervais!"

He yelled and searched till his voice gave out. In despair his knees suddenly bent under him as he fell exhausted to the ground. His hands clenched his hair as he buried his face in his knees. He whispered to himself: "What a wretch I am!"

His heart swelled and he burst into tears. It was the first time he had cried in two decades.

The gentle words of the bishop resonated in his

head, "you belong no longer to evil, but to good. It is your soul that I am buying for you. I withdraw it from dark thoughts and from the spirit of evil and I give it to God!"

Valjean knew he was no longer the same man, he was changed. He saw two men in his mind – the bishop, and the prisoner 24601. The image of the bishop grew bigger and brighter in his mind while 24601, the hideous galley-slave, shrank and faded away. In Valjean's mind, the bishop alone remained.

He walked all night back the way he had come. When he finally arrived at the door with no locks, he did not knock, he simply knelt down on the ground, and for the first time in his life, Jean Valjean prayed.

Chapter 5: Fantine

In the year 1817, a young man named Felix left Paris to go have a "season of fun." He was a rich young man whose parents gave him four thousand dollars a year. He was thirty years old and was full of jests, joy, and laughter. His rich, easy going manner made him seem dashingly handsome to all the young ladies he met, but only one girl managed to catch his eye. A young country girl named Fantine. All her friends called her "the blonde" on account of her beautiful hair. She fell instantly in love with Felix and knew that this was her first and only love. She was certain their love would be eternal. She didn't know that Felix saw it simply as a fun little fling.

For nearly two years they adored each other. They basked in the sunshine, picking the flowers, running in the fields, and climbing the trees. They spent hours singing, running, dancing, chasing butterflies, and stealing kisses from each other.

Then one day, after dinner, Felix told Fantine that he wanted to go and get her a surprise. He kissed her on the forehead and walked out of the Café.

She sat alone, anxiously waiting with her elbows on the table, trying to imagine what he might bring her. A dress? A horse? Oh! Maybe even a wedding ring? After nearly an hour the boy who had been their waiter at dinner came to her table and handed her a letter.

"What is that?" asked Fantine.

"It is a paper that the gentlemen left for you." he replied.

Fantine snatched the paper from his hands and read:

> *THIS IS THE SURPRISE.*
> *Oh, Fantine!*
> *My parents miss me and have begged me to return home. To be a good and virtuous son, I must obey. At the moment when you read this, I have already mounted my horse and am on my way back home to my parents. I am gone.*
>
> *FELIX THOLOMYES*
>
> *P. S. The dinner is paid for.*

Fantine ran home and wept bitterly. She cried so loud that she could hardly hear the screams of the baby. She had given herself to this Felix like a wife gives herself to a husband. The poor girl now had a child.

For nearly a year Fantine tried to make things work. She had been abandoned with no job, no skills, no training, no money, and a child but no husband. She was rejected by her friends and ridiculed by those around her. She desperately needed work but had no one to care for her child during working hours, so she begged instead. She soon found herself wandering from city to city with nothing but her child and a bag of clothes.

As she entered the town of Montfermeil one day, she saw two young girls playing in the street while their mother watched from a doorway. Fantine looked up and saw it was an old inn named THE SERGEANT OF WATERLOO.

Fantine looked back out at the two little girls. The children were well dressed, smiling with their sparkling eyes and their blooming, laughing faces.

The mother, a woman whose appearance was rather forbidding, appeared quite touching at this moment, as she stood in the doorway of the inn. While watching her young ones she sang a little lullaby. She didn't hear Fantine approaching until she heard a voice say quite near her:

"You have two pretty children there, madam."

The madam turned and saw a woman carrying a young child and a large carpet-bag. The child was one of the divinest beings that can be imagined: a little girl of two or three years. She wore a beautiful dress of fine linen and smiled with charmingly rosy cheeks.

The madam looked at Fantine and saw that her thick blonde hair was fastened up beneath an ugly bonnet. Her eyes were red from constant tears. She looked pale, weary and somewhat sick.

The madam at the inn offered her a seat.

"My name is Madam Thenardier," said the mother of the two girls. "My husband and I own this inn."

As they spoke, Fantine told her story, though a bit modified.

She said she was a working woman, and her husband was dead. Not being able to find work in her home town she was going in search of it elsewhere.

At this moment her child awoke and began to laugh and squirmed out of her mother's arms.

Madam Thenardier called to her two daughters: "Play together, all three of you."

The two women continued to chat.

"What do you call your brat?" asked Madam Thenardier.

"Cosette."

"How old is she?"

"She is going on three years."

"That's the age of my oldest, Eponine. Her sister there is Azelma."

The three young girls were giggling and smiling as if they had known each other for ages.

"Children," exclaimed Madam Thenardier, "how soon they know one another. See them! One would swear they were three sisters."

These words put an idea into Fantine's head and she blurted it out instantly:

"Will you keep my child for me?"

Madam Thenardier looked at her in shock.

"I cannot take my child with me," Fantine continued. "Work forbids it. It is God who has led me to your inn. I see your little ones, so pretty, and clean, and happy. You are a good mother; they will be like three sisters, and then it will not be long before I come back. I'll pay for all her expenses. Will you keep my child for me?"

"I must think over it," said Thenardier.

"I can pay six dollars a month," pled Fantine.

Suddenly a man's voice was heard from within the Inn:

"Not less than seven dollars, and six months paid in advance."

"That is my husband," said Madam Thenardier.

"I will give it," said Fantine.

"And fifteen dollars extra for the first expenses," added the husband.

"That's fifty-seven dollars," said Madam Thenardier.

"I will give it," said Fantine. "I will go to work, earn some more money, and as soon as I have enough to care for her I will come for my little love."

"Deal" said the husband.

The bargain was made. Fantine stayed that night at their inn, gave her money to the Thenardiers, and the next morning left her child behind as she left to seek work.

When Fantine had gone, Mr. Thenardier said to his wife:

"That money came just in time. I was fifty dollars short. I would have had the sheriff after me by Monday. You've turned out to be a good mousetrap with our little ones."

CHAPTER 6: THE MAYOR OF MON-SUR-MER

After leaving her little Cosette with the Thenardiers, Fantine travelled to the city of Mon-sur-mer. It was 1818 and the city was booming with business. Everyone had jobs and the citizens all seemed happy and healthy.

This was all due to an unknown man who had moved there in 1815. He had entered the little city of Mon-sur-mer at dusk on a December evening when a great fire broke out in a town-house. This visitor rushed into the fire and saved two children, whose father turned out to be the police captain. In the hurry and gratitude of the moment, no one thought to ask the stranger for his passport. From that time on he had simply been known by the name of *Father Madeleine*.

Father Madeleine quickly found work making bracelets in a local factory. After a few months he had the idea that instead of buying expensive clasps for each bracelet, he could make the clasps himself by simply bending the ends of the metal together.

This very slight change made a huge difference. It made the production of bracelets cheaper, raising the profits so that the factory and its workers made a fortune.

In less than three years the inventor of this process had become rich. Through hard work and creative ideas, he had made most everyone in the city rich as well. Father Madeleine's name was known by everyone, but he was still a stranger in town. Nobody knew where he was born or where he had come from.

He employed everybody in his factory and had only one condition which he repeated often, "Be an honest man! Be an honest woman!"

Father Madeleine thought often of others, and seldom of himself. By 1820 he had saved $630,000 for himself, but only after donating a million dollars to the city and its poor.

He made the city so rich, and the people so happy, that the king of France appointed him the mayor of the city.

Thus, Father Madeleine became Mayor Madeleine.

When Fantine came to town looking for work she was hired to work in his factory. She didn't make a lot for her day's work; but the little she did earn was enough. Her life was looking up. She was earning a living doing honest work. She would soon be able to save enough to go and get her precious daughter Cosette.

CHAPTER 7: JAVERT

Everyone in Mon-sur-mer loved and revered their mayor. Well, almost everyone. There was one man who didn't seem to trust the mayor. He was a tall man who always wore a flat hat and an iron-grey coat. His name was Inspector Javert. Every time he passed the mayor in the street, he would stop and think "I recognize that man from somewhere."

Javert was a hard man. He had been born in a prison. His mother was a fortune-teller and his father was a convict. Javert hated his mother and all the gypsies. He hated his father and all criminals. He himself had become a policeman. He did his job so well that by the age of forty he was already an inspector.

This man, Inspector Javert, always had an eye fixed on Mayor Madeleine; an eye full of suspicion.

One day, his suspicion was confirmed.

As Mayor Madeleine was walking the unpaved alleys of Mon-sur-mer; he heard a shouting and saw a crowd. An old man named Fosh was trapped under a cart. His horse had broken its legs and could not stand. The old man was caught beneath the cart with the whole weight resting on his chest. The cart was heavily loaded, and Fosh groaned in agony. The people tried to pull him out, but their attempts were in vain.

Javert arrived just after the accident had occurred

and sent for a jack to lift the cart.

Mayor Madeleine arrived soon after and the crowd fell back with respect.

"Help," cried old Fosh from beneath the cart.

Mayor Madeleine turned towards the bystanders:

"Does anyone have a jack?"

"They have gone for one," replied a peasant.

"How soon will it be here?"

"Fifteen minutes at least."

"He'll be dead in fifteen minutes!" cried the mayor.

It had rained the night before. The road was soft and the cart was sinking deeper and deeper into the mud, pressing harder and harder on the chest of Fosh. In less than five minutes his ribs would be crushed.

"We cannot wait for the jack," said Mayor Madeleine to the peasants who were looking on. "Listen, there is room enough still under the wagon for a man to crawl in, and lift it with his back. In half a minute we will have the poor man out. Is there nobody here who has strength and courage? One hundred dollars for him!"

"Impossible," a voice called out. "I have known but one man capable of doing what you call for."

The mayor turned and saw that it was Javert speaking.

"That man was a convict in the prison at Toulon," he continued. "No one here has that strength. It's impossible."

Madeleine became pale and looked at Javert with fear. The cart was sinking lower as Fosh wailed and screamed:

"I am dying! My ribs are breaking! A jack! Anything! Please!"

Madeleine felt the falcon eye of Javert still fixed upon him. Then, without saying a word, the mayor fell to the ground and shimmied his way under the cart. The bystanders started to cry out, but then stopped to watch in an awful moment of suspense and silence.

Madeleine, lying almost flat under the heavy cart, tried twice to get his elbows and knees under him so he could lift. Both times he failed.

The people cried out to him: "Mayor Madeleine! Come out from there!"

Old Fosh himself said: "Mayor Madeleine! Go away! I must die; you see that; leave me! You will be crushed too."

Madeleine made no answer. The bystanders held their breath. The wheels were still sinking and now Mayor Madeleine himself would not be able to escape.

All at once the enormous cart started to rise, the wheels came half out of the ruts. A smothered voice was heard, crying: "Quick! Help!" It was Madeleine, who had just made a final effort and had lifted the entire cart on his back.

The bystanders all rushed in to help. The cart was lifted by twenty arms. Fosh was pulled to safety.

The mayor crawled out, dripping with sweat. His clothes were torn and covered with mud as he stood and everyone surrounded him weeping and praising him. Fosh kissed the mayor and called him a godsend. The Mayor himself wore a smile of joy, until he looked at Javert. Javert was glaring at him more than ever.

Chapter 8: The Descent

The mayor continued his life as if nothing had changed.

He gave Fosh a thousand dollars, and when his broken bones were healed, the mayor found him a more relaxing job as a gardener at a convent in Paris.

The Mayor went about doing good; occasionally checking in on his factory to make sure the foreman was keeping things in line.

Fantine was still working there, but things were not going well for her. The other women in the factory were gossipers and busybodies. They had set their eyes on Fantine and now they were determined to learn her secrets. They knew she wrote secret letters and many were jealous of her beautiful hair and perfect white teeth.

The women eventually figured out that she wrote The mayor continued his life as if nothing had changed.

He gave Fosh a thousand dollars, and when his broken bones were healed, the mayor found him a more relaxing job as a gardener at a convent in Paris.

The Mayor went about doing good; occasionally checking in on his factory to make sure the foreman was keeping things in line.

Fantine was still working there, but things were not going well for her. The other women in the factory were gossipers and busybodies. They had set their eyes on Fantine and now they were determined to learn her secrets. They knew she wrote secret letters and many were jealous of her beautiful hair and perfect white teeth.

The women eventually figured out that she wrote at least twice a month to an innkeeper named Thenardier in a town called Montfermeil. Then they also found out that Fantine had a child.

"Ah, she must be *that* sort of a woman" they said.

By the time the women of the factory found all this out, an entire year had passed.

Fantine had been told by the Thenardiers that Cosette was not well, but she did not know even half of the horrors her daughter had endured.

The Thenardiers had used Fantine's fifty-seven dollars to stay out of jail. The next month they were still in need of money, so the madam sold all of Cosette's clothes and dressed her in rags. They fed her nothing but leftover scraps. The dog and cat were her only friends. Cosette ate her meals with them under the table in a wooden dish, just like theirs.

Every few months the Thenardiers asked for more money; first twelve dollars a month, then fifteen. Soon they were asking for more money than Fantine could pay and she fell behind in her payments.

Cosette was now five years old, and since Fantine wasn't paying the new price, the Thenardiers made Cosette their servant. She was forced to run errands, sweep the rooms, wash the dishes, and carry the heaviest burdens. It was winter time and the poor child, not yet six years old, was seen every day, shivering in her torn clothing, sweeping the street before daylight. She had an enormous broom in her little red hands and tears in her large eyes.

It was in the middle of this fierce winter that Fantine arrived to work one day only to find that she'd been fired. No explanation was given; she was simply tossed out into the street.

Fantine now couldn't pay for her daughter or for herself. Overwhelmed with shame and despair, she left the workshop, and walked slowly home to her apartment.

Mayor Madeleine knew nothing of all this. He had placed a woman in charge of his shop and he trusted her judgment. When she recommended firing Fantine, the mayor assumed she had good reasons.

Fantine was forced to do whatever work she could find. She offered herself as a servant in the neighborhood and knocked at every door asking if she could do some chores. She worked hard, but still earned too little. The Thenardiers were now writing her weekly berating her and demanding their money. They told her Cosette was completely out of clothing and that she would freeze in the cold winter weather. They demanded ten dollars immediately to buy Cosette a thick wool skirt. Fantine cried over the letter for an entire day, thinking of her poor daughter freezing to death. In the evening she went into a barbershop and pulled out her hairclip. Her beautiful blonde hair shined all the way to her waist.

"What beautiful hair!" exclaimed the barber.

"How much will you give me for it?" she asked.

"Ten dollars."

"Then cut it off."

Fantine bought a $10 wool skirt and sent it to the Thenardiers.

Fantine thought to herself: "My child is no longer cold; I have clothed her with my hair."

The skirt made the Thenardiers furious. It was the money they had wanted. They gave the skirt to their own daughter Eponine and left Cosette still shivering in the cold.

The next week Fantine received a letter from the Thenardiers that said "Cosette is sick with a deadly fever. The medicine is very expensive and we can't afford it. Unless you send us forty dollars this week, your little one will die."

Fantine burst out in tears. Where could she get forty dollars? She didn't even have forty cents!

Fantine ran down the staircase and out into the street. As she passed through the square, she saw many people gathered around a traveling dentist who was offering to the public complete sets of teeth.

Fantine looked at the table full of teeth and as she did the dentist noticed her beautiful white teeth.

"Madam," he said, "If you will sell me your two incisors, I will give you twenty dollars for each of them."

"What is that? What are my incisors?" asked Fantine.

"They are the front teeth, the two upper ones."

"How horrible!" cried Fantine.

"Forty dollars!" grumbled a toothless old hag who stood nearby. "How lucky she is!"

The next morning Fantine arrived at the post office. She stood in line, bald, pale, and coughing. The woman at the counter noticed dried blood at the corners of her mouth. Fantine mailed the $40 to the Thenardiers and said "Now my child will not die with that deadly fever. I have saved her with my smile." As Fantine smiled a dark bloody hole was visible where her front two teeth had been.

That night Fantine threw her mirror out the window. She couldn't bear the sight of herself. She had no hair, no front teeth, no real clothes; she no longer even had a bed, just a mattress on the floor. She had lost everything. She cried herself to sleep each night thinking of Cosette.

The next week the Thenardiers wrote to her again saying that they were being too generous and that they must now have a hundred dollars immediately, or else little Cosette, just recovering from her severe sickness, would be turned out into the cold streets of winter, likely to die.

The letters were all lies. Cosette had never been sick but Fantine had no way of knowing that. She sat in silent horror. "A hundred dollars," thought Fantine. "Where is there a place where one can earn a hundred dollars?"

Her mind at last turned to an option she had

never considered in her life.

"Come!" she said, "I will sell what is left."

The unfortunate creature became a woman of the town.

Chapter 9: Intervention

In the early part of January, 1823; on an evening when it had been snowing; a young man was amusing himself. He was a "dandy," dressed in a warm and comfortable coat, and he was tormenting a young woman who was walking back and forth in front of a café. She was dressed in a torn ball gown, with her neck and shoulders bare.

Every time that the woman passed before him, he would yell out an insult: "How ugly you are!" "Are you bald?" "You have lost your teeth!"

As she passed by him again he snuck up silently behind her and, stifling his laughter, threw a handful of snow down her back between her naked shoulders. The woman roared with rage and turned and jumped at him like a panther, burying her nails in his face and spewing forth the most foul language imaginable. The woman was Fantine.

At the sound of her cursing and the dandy's screaming, a crowd quickly gathered and watched as the man defended himself against this raging horror of a woman. They cheered as the toothless bald prostitute kicked and scratched at the young dandy.

Suddenly a tall man stepped out from the crowd, seized the woman by her muddy waist, and said: "Come with me!"

The woman raised her head; her furious voice dying out at once. Her eyes were glassy and she had become pale. She shuddered with terror as she saw who had grabbed her, it was Inspector Javert.

The dandy took advantage of this moment to sneak away.

Javert walked her into the police station, dropped her in the corner and said to a Sergeant: "Take three men, and carry this girl to jail." Then turning to Fantine he added: "You are in for six months."

"Six months? Six months in prison?" she cried. "But what will become of Cosette? My daughter! My daughter! Sir Javert, I beg your pity. That man threw snow down my back. That made me wild. Have pity on me. If I go to prison my little Cosette will die. Please sir Javert."

He looked over at her, shaking with sobs, blinded by tears, coughing miserably.

"Sergeant," said Javert, "March off at once! I said six months!"

The soldiers seized Fantine by the arms.

"One moment, if you please!" said an authoritative voice from the corner.

A man had entered the room without being noticed. Javert raised his eyes and recognized Mayor Madeleine. Javert took off his hat, and bowed saying: "Pardon, Mayor Madeleine"

Fantine, hearing the Mayor's name and remembering that he had fired her and thrust her into this awful life, sprang to her feet and spit in the mayor's face.

Mayor Madeleine wiped his face and said:

"Inspector Javert set this woman free."

Javert was astounded.

"Sir Mayor that cannot be done."

"Why?" said Mayor Madeleine.

"This wretched woman has insulted a citizen."

"I was passing through the square when you arrested this woman; there was a crowd still there and I learned what really happened. It was the dandy who was in the wrong."

Javert interrupted the mayor saying "But now this wretch has just spit in your face. I cannot allow this injustice. I am very sorry to resist the Mayor; it is the first time in my life, but I am the Inspector of the Police, and I order that she go to jail."

At this Mayor Madeleine folded his arms and said in a severe tone which nobody in the city had ever yet heard:

"By the criminal code of France, articles nine, eleven, fifteen, and sixty-six; I, the mayor, have the final say in these matters. I order that this woman be set at liberty."

Javert stared at the Mayor angrily. He did not like to lose. He attempted one more time to speak:

"Mayor, please permit-"

"LEAVE NOW," said Mayor Madeleine.

Javert bowed to the ground before the mayor, and went out.

When Javert was gone, Mayor Madeleine turned towards Fantine and said to her, speaking slowly: "I will care for you now. I heard you owe money to get your daughter back? I will pay your debts; I will have your child brought to you. You are a good woman, a caring mother. I have no doubt that you have never ceased to be a virtuous and holy woman before God."

Fantine could not believe what she was hearing. She would have Cosette back. She could leave this nightmare of a life! She was so overwhelmed that her legs collapsed and she fainted into the mayor's arms.

CHAPTER 10: A TEMPEST IN THE BRAIN

That very night, two letters were written: one from Javert to the Prefecture of Police in Paris, the other from Mayor Madeleine to the Thenardiers. Fantine believed she owed them a $120. Madeleine sent them $300 and instructed them to bring the child at once to Mon-sur-mer, where her mother, who was sick, wanted her.

Mr. Thenardier licked his lips when the letter arrived. He kept the $300 and quickly wrote up a bill for fake medical expenses and requested another $300.

Mayor Madeleine immediately sent the money and wrote: "Make haste to bring Cosette."

Thenardier was shocked. $600 in one week? He was never letting Cosette go now; she was his key to a fortune.

While the mayor begged for Cosette to be brought to town, Fantine kept getting worse. She was in the hospital begging daily to see her daughter.

Mayor Madeleine wrote more letters, but each time the Thenardiers gave a hundred excuses why Cosette couldn't travel.

Finally, Mayor Madeleine decided to go retrieve the child himself.

Fantine wrote a letter for him stating:

Sir Thenardier:
You will deliver Cosette to the bearer of this letter.
He will settle all debts.

FANTINE

The next morning as the mayor prepared to go to Montfermeil to get Cosette, Javert knocked at his door.

The mayor asked hurriedly: "Well, what is it? What is the matter, Javert?"

Javert remained silent a moment as if collecting himself; then raised his voice and said:

"I come to resign as Inspector, and to be charged with a crime."

The mayor looked at him in surprise: "What have you done?"

"Six weeks ago, after that scene about that girl, I was enraged and I denounced you."

"Denounced me?"

"To the Prefecture of Police at Paris. I told them you were a former convict who had broken his parole. When I saw your immense strength lifting the cart off old Fosh; I was sure that you were a convict named Jean Valjean."

"What was that name? Asked the Mayor.

"Jean Valjean. He was a convict I saw twenty years ago, when I was a guard at Toulon. After leaving prison this man robbed a bishop's palace, then he stole from a little boy on the highway. For eight years his whereabouts have been unknown, and we've been searching for him. When I saw your strength, I was certain you were that man, and I denounced you."

"What did the prefect say?"

"That I was crazy," answered Javert. "And they were right, for the real Jean Valjean has been found."

"What?" Asked Mayor Madeleine in a strained voice.

"In the city of Arras there was a fellow called Champmathieu. He stole some fruit and was arrested. When they put him in the prison three separate prisoners all recognized him from serving time in Toulon together. They said he was Jean Valjean. The thief denied it all, but it was obvious to everyone. When the Prefecture of Police told me this, I couldn't believe it, so I went to Arras to see myself."

"And?" interrupted Mayor Madeleine.

"Sir Mayor, truth is truth. I am sorry for it, but that man is Jean Valjean. I recognized him too."

Mayor Madeleine said in a very low voice: "Are you sure?"

"Without a doubt," Javert replied. "The case will be tried tomorrow; I leave tonight so I can testify."

Mayor Madeleine paused and eventually said "Very well" and dismissed Javert with a wave of his hand.

Javert did not go.

"Sir, I have wronged you, I ought to be dismissed from the Police force."

"Javert, you are a man of honor and I respect you.

You exaggerate your fault. Keep your post."

"Yes Sir," said Javert and he turned and went out.

As soon as he was out of sight Mayor Madeleine ran out of the room and went directly to the stables and reserved a horse and carriage for the next morning at 4:30 a.m.

Mayor Madeleine then went home and sat down to think.

I have been doing good for years now. I have been helping people. I am an honest and good man, a mayor! I have closed the door on my past. Must I save this stranger and go back to prison? Do I have to be Valjean again? No. This is my way out. This is God granting me freedom. This other 'Jean Valjean' will go to prison, and I will be free forever.

At that moment he looked above the fireplace and saw the two massive silver candlesticks he had been given by the Bishop. He remembered the bishop, and his promise to God. He knew what he must do. He must go to Arras, confess, and set the other man free.

"Well," he said, "Let us do our duty! Let us save this man!"

Then he thought of Fantine.

"Stop!" he said, "this poor woman!"

If Jean Valjean went to prison, no one would save Cosette. No one would care for Fantine. He had made a promise to her to bring her Cosette.

I must think of others, not just myself. I am a mayor, and I run the factory that supports the town. Without me it will all fall apart. Everyone will be poor again, and I will have to break my promise to this poor woman who has suffered so much. No. I must stay here. If God wants to save that other man who looks like me, it is in God's hands. I must keep my promises.

He stood up to undress and go to bed when he thought he heard a voice in his head. He turned around and looked at the candlesticks again. He seemed to hear the Bishop calling to him:

"Have you forgotten me, forgotten everything? Will you really stay here, comfortable and rich while another man goes to prison for you? Will you really let him wear your red blouse, bear your name and drag your chain in prison? You evil wretch!"

The voice went silent as Valjean carefully placed the candlesticks back on the mantel and ran out the door toward the stables.

CHAPTER 11:THE TRIAL

Valjean rode through the night and the entire next day to get to Arras.

He arrived at the courthouse and was told there was no more room, the entire courtroom was full.

He told the officer at the door that he was a local magistrate, a mayor, and that he therefore had a right to sit in the privileged seats behind the judge.

Valjean was admitted and took his reserved seat. He looked at the defendants table and thought he saw himself. A man sat there who looked just like Valjean had eight years ago, with that bristling hair, those wild and restless eyes and that red blouse.

Valjean looked for Javert but did not see him. He had already given his testimony and gone home.

Valjean listened as the prosecutor said: "We have here not merely a fruit thief, but a bandit; an outlaw who has broken his parole; an old convict called Jean Valjean. Four witnesses have positively and without hesitation identified Champmathieu as the galley slave, Jean Valjean. Javert, the inspector of police; and three old prison cell-mates, the convicts Brevet, Chenil, and Coche. The case is clear, your honor. This man is Jean Valjean. Find him guilty, and send him away."

At this moment a loud voice was heard from behind the judge:

"Brevet, Chenil, Coche, look this way!"

So rough and terrible was this voice that those who heard it felt their blood run cold. All eyes turned to see the source of the voice, it was Mayor Madeleine.

"Gentlemen of the jury, release the accused" the mayor demanded. "Your honor, order my arrest. He is not the man whom you seek; it is I. I am Jean Valjean."

The court erupted in surprise and the judge thundered his gavel crying "Order, order."

Valjean advanced towards the witnesses.

"Do you recognize me?"

All three convicts stood confused and shook their heads.

"Well! I recognize each of you. Brevet, your entire left shoulder is badly burned and scarred from the day you tried to attack me near the furnace. Answer me, is this true?"

"It is true!" said Brevet in shock.

Valjean turned to Coche:

"Coche, you have on your left arm, a tattoo. It is the date that Emperor Napoleon landed at Cannes, March 1st, 1815. Lift up your sleeve. Show the court!

Coche lifted up his sleeve; the date was there.

Valjean turned towards the audience and the court: "You see clearly," he said, "that I am Jean Valjean. Since I haven't yet been arrested, and have many things to do, I will leave. The prosecuting attorney knows where I live, and will have me arrested when he chooses."

Valjean walked briskly towards the door. Not a voice was raised and not a single arm stretched out to prevent him.

A few minutes later Champmathieu was declared innocent and was set free.

Chapter 12: Order Restored

Day began to dawn. Fantine had had a feverish and sleepless night and was finally dozing off when Valjean arrived, breathless at her bedside.

She opened her eyes, saw him, and asked with a smile:

"Where's Cosette? Did you bring her? Oh, let me see her. I can't wait any longer to see her angelic face and her- "

Suddenly she ceased speaking. Valjean raised his head to look at her – She had become frail and white. She did not speak; she did not breathe, her eyes fixed on something across the room.

"What is it, Fantine?" Valjean asked.

She did not answer; she raised her hand to point across the room.

Valjean turned and saw Javert glaring at him with the face of a demon.

Javert smiled in victory as Fantine cried out "Mayor Madeleine, save me!"

Jean Valjean said to Fantine in his gentlest and calmest tone:

"Be at peace, it is not for you that he comes."

Javert called out to Valjean: "Come now, don't' make me get the chains."

Fantine saw Javert seize the Mayor by the collar and the mayor bowed his head in surrender.

"But… Sir the Mayor, what is this? What's

happening?"

Javert burst into a horrid laugh.

"There is no *Sir the Mayor* here any longer! He is a convict; a thief; a fake."

"Please Javert," Valjean whispered. "I need three days! Three days to go for the child of this poor woman! I will pay whatever is necessary. You can go with me if you like."

"Speak up when you talk to me!" shouted Javert. "And call me Inspector! Do you think I'm stupid? You ask for three days to get away. You've run before, you'll run again. You think I'll let you go get this woman's child?"

Fantine shivered.

"My child!" she exclaimed, "Where is Cosette? I want my child! Sir Madeleine, Sir the Mayor!"

Javert stamped his foot.

"Hold your tongue, hussy! I tell you that there is no Sir Madeleine, and that there is no Sir the Mayor. There is a robber, a convict called Jean Valjean, and I have got him! That is what there is!"

Fantine tried to sit up. She opened her mouth as if to speak but only a rattle came from her throat. Her teeth slammed together as her body jerked backwards. She stretched out her arms in anguish; then sank suddenly back upon the pillow. Her head struck the headboard of the bed and her mouth gaped open as her eyes glazed over.

She was dead.

Jean Valjean whispered coldly: "You have killed

this woman."

"I am not here to listen to sermons" spat Javert. "Come right along, or the handcuffs!"

In a corner of the room there stood an old iron bed. Jean Valjean went to the bed, tore from it an iron bar with his massive hands and glared at Javert with clenched fists. Javert recoiled towards the door.

Jean Valjean, the iron bar in hand, walked slowly towards the bed of Fantine. On reaching it, he turned and said to Javert:

"Do not disturb me now, or it will end badly for you."

Jean Valjean took Fantine's head in his hands and arranged it on the pillow, as a mother would have done for her child. He fixed her hair, and laid her arms by her sides. Then he closed her eyes and took her hand. He gently raised it to his lips and kissed it softly.

Then he turned to Javert:

"You have killed this woman and would have her daughter die as well. You will leave this house right now. Chase me, find me, do what you must, but you best bring all your men because I have made this woman a promise, and I will die before I break it."

Javert bowed out of the room and ran to collect his men.

Valjean ran home and packed his money, a few clothes and the two silver candlesticks.

By the time Javert returned, Valjean was already out the door and on his way to Montfermeil.

PART TWO: COSETTE

CHAPTER 1: THE THENARDIERS

Madam Thenardier was red-faced, freckled and fat. Little Cosette looked like a mouse in the service of an elephant. Everything trembled at the sound of Madam Thenardier's voice.

Mr. Thenardier was small, pale and bony with the look of a weasel. He smoked a large pipe and pretended to be a man of literature. He told everyone that he was a great war hero; that he had been a sergeant in Napoleon's army and he had personally rescued a wounded General during the Battle of Waterloo.

In reality, Thenardier had been a thief, one of the worst kinds. He had never joined the army, but the day after the Battle of Waterloo he had snuck out on the battlefield and searched the dead bodies for money or valuables. After stealing one officer's wallet and watch he saw that the corpse also wore a gold ring. Thenardier had tried to slide the ring off the officer's finger, but it was stuck. As Thenardier pulled harder he had suddenly felt the officer's finger move. Thenardier fell to the ground in shock as the officer that he thought was dead, opened his eyes.

"Thank you for finding me," said the officer feebly. "If you hadn't tried to pull me to safety, I would have died right here. You have saved my life. What is your name?"

"Thenardier."

"I shall not forget that name," said the officer. "And you; you remember my name: Sergeant Pontmercy."

When Thenardier told the story, he said that he himself was a Sergeant who had found a wounded General, and while being fired at by a thousand enemy soldiers he had carried the General to safety. He had painted a picture of the event and hung it over the door to his inn. He had even named the Inn: "The Sergeant of Waterloo."

This was the man that Cosette found herself a slave to; him and his beastly bride.

On one particularly cold evening Madam Thenardier ordered Cosette to go get more water from the well in the woods.

Cosette grabbed the bucket and hurried out the door, but she stopped when she saw the brightly lit window of the toy-shop across the street. In the window stood a doll nearly two feet tall, with real hair and enamel eyes, dressed in a pretty pink robe. Every little girl in town had begged for that doll, including Eponine and Azelma. But no one in town was rich enough to afford the doll, so there it sat in the window, day after day.

Suddenly Cosette heard the harsh voice of the madam: "Still here? Be off little monster!"

Cosette fled with her bucket, running as fast as she could with tears in her eyes.

She filled the bucket and tried to hurry back to the inn, but the bucket was far too heavy and her cold feet slipped on the icy ground. She began to cry even more as she knew she was taking too long, and she'd be beaten the moment she got back.

While crying in despair she felt the bucket lift up out of her hand as if it were weightless. She looked up and saw a giant hand on the bucket handle. A large man was walking next to her, carrying the bucket with ease.

"Little girl, how old are you?" he asked.

"Eight years Sir," she said, wiping the tears away.

"And what is your name?" asked the man.

"Cosette."

The man stopped suddenly as if he'd been shot. He looked at her again, more closely this time, then continued on.

"Who sent you out into the woods at this time of night?"

"Madam Thenardier. She keeps the inn."

"Is there no one else at the inn to get the water?"

"There are her two little girls. Eponine and Azelma, but they play."

"And you?"

"Me! I work."

"All day long?"

"Yes, Sir," she said with a tear in her eye.

When they reached the door of the inn Cosette asked if she could carry the bucket again.

"What for?" the man asked.

"Because if madam sees that anybody helped me, she will beat me."

The man gave her the bucket and they walked inside.

Chapter 2: Bartering with a Beggar

"Oh! It is you, you little beggar! You certainly took your time!" bellowed the madam as Cosette entered. Then she saw the man and quickly changed her tone of voice as she sweetly said:

"Enter, good man."

The "good man" entered as Cosette crawled under a table and started knitting. Eponine and Azelma were sitting across from her, carrying a doll they loved to play with. Cosette stared at the doll longingly.

Madam Thenardier noticed and cried out: "Slacking again are you? I'll make you work I will" as she turned and reached for the whip.

"Madam," said the stranger, smiling. "Let her play!"

The madam replied sharply: "I don't feed her for free. She knits those stalking to pay for her food."

"Then let me pay for her time. Those stalking couldn't be worth more than 50 cents. I'll give you five dollars so that she can play."

Both Thenardiers looked at the man in shock. What sort of man paid five dollars to watch a little girl play?

Cosette trembled as she asked:

"Madam, is it true? Can I play?"

Mr. Thenardier now spoke up: "Sir," he said, to

the stranger, "I am very happy that the child should play, but she must be taught to work if she is to survive this life."

"The child is not yours, then?" asked the man.

Madam Thenardier answered "Oh no, Sir! She's a little beggar that we have taken in through charity. For six months we haven't heard from her mother, she's probably dead. Good riddance, she was no great woman, abandoning her child like she did."

The strangers hand curled into a fist, but he stayed silent.

Eponine and Azelma had dropped their doll and were now playing with the dog. When they turned back around they saw that Cosette had picked up their doll. They screamed for their mother.

Madam Thenardier turned and shrieked with a harsh voice:

"Cosette!"

The traveler arose.

"What is the matter?" he asked Madam Thenardier.

"That beggar," answered the madam, "has dared to touch my children's doll."

The man walked straight to the inn door, opened it, and went out.

As soon as he had gone, Madam Thenardier kicked Cosette under the table.

The door opened again, and the man walked back in carrying the fabulous doll from the toy shop across the street. He bent down and handed it to Cosette.

Cosette raised her swollen tearful eyes; looked at the doll, then embraced it and said proudly: "I will call her Catherine."

All four Thenardiers froze like statues.

"That doll cost at least thirty dollars." Mr. Thenardier whispered to his wife, "No nonsense now. Down on your knees before that millionaire. Give him anything he wants. He could make us rich tonight!"

The madam immediately stopped yelling at Cosette. She was now kind and sweet and offered the stranger anything he could want: more dinner, a pillow, a room for the night, music.

The stranger ignored her completely. He finished his meal and stood, picking up his coat.

"Are you going to leave us already?" asked the madam nervously.

"Yes, madam. What do I owe for the dinner?"

She looked at her husband who quickly pulled out a paper to write up a bill.

She turned back to the stranger and lamented.

"Oh! Sir, the times are very hard, and we are very poor. If we only had rich travelers now and then, like you Sir! We have so many expenses! Why, that little girl eats us out of house and home."

"Suppose you were relieved of her?" he asked.

"Who? Cosette?" The red and violent face of the woman lit up with joy as she realized his meaning.

"Oh yes sir! Take her, keep her, carry her off!"

"Agreed," the stranger said immediately.

"Really! You will take her away?"

"I will."

At that moment Mr. Thenardier suddenly interrupted.

"Sir, I must say that I adore this child. Oh, our dear little Cosette! You wish to take her away from us? I cannot allow it. I should miss her too much. We are not rich, but we Christians must do what is right before God."

"And what is that?" asked the stranger.

Thenardier sat in deep thought as he weighed his options. Should he pretend to be a good Christian, or just come right out and ask for the money he wanted?

"Sir," Thenardier said at last, "I must have fifteen hundred dollars for her."

The stranger instantly took out his wallet and drew out fifteen $100 bills and placed them on the table.

"Bring Cosette. Now," the stranger commanded.

Thenardier whispered to his wife:

"This man is a millionaire, and I'm letting him go for a mere $1500. We can't let him go yet, not till we get every cent he has."

Then Thenardier turned to the stranger:

"I'm an honest man, I can't accept your small bribe because the little girl is not mine. She belongs to her mother. Even if her mother is dead I cannot do it. I can only give Cosette to her rightful guardian. No sir, you cannot have her."

The stranger without answering, felt in his pocket,

and Thenardier saw him draw out his wallet once again.

The inn-keeper felt a thrill of joy.

"Good!" thought he; "Here comes the full load, maybe thousands, maybe millions!"

The stranger pulled out a little piece of paper, which he unfolded and showed to the inn-keeper.

"Sir, you are right." The man said as he handed Thenardier the paper.

Thenardier took it and read. -

Sir Thenardier:

You will deliver Cosette to the bearer of this letter. He will settle all debts.

FANTINE

The stranger was Jean Valjean. He stood, and motioned for Cosette to come over by his side.

Thenardier tried one last time: "Sir," he said, "It says you must settle 'all debts.' There is a large amount due to me."

Valjean rose to his feet and said sternly:

"Sir Thenardier, you received $300 a few weeks ago and another $300 the week after that. I have just given you $1500. The debt is more than paid."

Valjean extended his hand to the little girl and said "Come, Cosette." Valjean took her little hand and together they walked out of the inn, never to return.

CHAPTER 3: THE DAWN OF LOVE

Valjean fumbled in his waistcoat and took from it a key, opened the rusted door in front of him, entered, then carefully closed the door again and went up the stairs, still carrying Cosette.

The room he had rented was furnished only with a mattress spread on the floor, a table, and a few chairs. Valjean laid the child down on the mattress without waking her, and bent down and kissed the child's hand.

A few months before, he had kissed the hand of her mother as she went to sleep for the last time.

They had arrived in Paris that morning, and Valjean had found the most abandoned part of town possible to rent a room. Cosette slept all morning until a big heavy wagon rumbled over the cobblestone road outside and shook the old building.

"Yes, Madam!" cried Cosette, starting up out of sleep. "Here I am! Here I am!"

Cosette jumped up from the mattress stretching out her hand towards the corner of the wall.

"Oh! What shall I do? Where is my broom?" she said.

By this time her eyes were fully open, and she saw the smiling face of Jean Valjean.

"Oh! yes- I forgot!" said the child. "Good morning, Sir."

Cosette noticed her doll, Catherine, at the foot of

the bed, and grabbed her at once to start playing. She then began asking Jean Valjean a thousand questions. - Where were they? Was Paris a big place? Was Madam Thenardier really, really far away? Would she come back again?

Thus, the day passed by; Cosette gradually forgetting her past as she played with her doll Catherine.

The dawn of the next day found Jean Valjean again near the bed of Cosette. He waited there, motionless, to see her awake.

Something new was entering his soul.

Jean Valjean had never loved anything. For twenty-five years he had been alone in the world. He had never been a father, a husband, or really even a friend. In prison he had grown angry, stubborn and short tempered.

Now, when he saw Cosette, he felt his heart moved. All the caring and loving feelings that could have ever existed in him were awakened by this child. He would approach the bed where she slept, and would tremble there with delight; he felt like a mother, and he was completely confused by the feelings he had. He did not recognize the feeling, because this was the first time he had ever felt love.

This was the second dawn of his life. The bishop had caused the dawn of virtue; Cosette evoked the dawn of love.

Weeks rolled by. From morning till nightfall Cosette laughed, joked and sang. Sometimes it happened that Jean Valjean would take her little red hand, all chapped and frost-bitten as it still was, and kiss it. The poor child, used to being hit all the time, didn't know how to respond.

Valjean began teaching her how to read. Sometimes, while teaching the child to spell, he would remember the days in prison he had spent learning to read. Back then he was doing it so he could learn to hurt others, to trick them, and to steal from them. Now he was using his skill for good, to teach his new love to read. The old convict would smile when he realized the transformation within him.

To teach Cosette to read and to watch her playing was nearly all of Jean Valjean's life now. He taught her to love, to read, and to pray. She called him Father, and knew him by no other name.

CHAPTER 4: THE BEGGAR WHO GIVES ALMS

Jean Valjean never went out in the daytime. He was too afraid that a policeman or the Thenardiers were chasing him. Every evening, however, about twilight, he would walk for an hour or two, sometimes alone, sometimes with Cosette, and visit the churches nearby.

They spent very little money, living as if they were poor. Valjean still wore his rough yellow coat, his black pants, and his old hat. On the street, everyone thought he was a beggar. Whenever Valjean met another beggar, much worse off than himself, he would quickly and quietly walk up to the beggar, slip a silver coin into his hand, and walk rapidly away. His generosity caused him some trouble, for word quickly spread, and he became known as the beggar who gives alms.

There was, in this neighborhood, a crippled beggar who sat at the same corner every day. Valjean passed by his corner often, always giving him at least a few pennies.

One evening, as Jean Valjean was passing that way, he noticed the beggar sitting in his usual place, under a street lamp. Valjean walked up to him, and put a piece of money in his hand like always. The beggar suddenly raised his eyes staring intently at Valjean, and then quickly dropped his head again.

Valjean shuddered and backed away quickly. The face he had seen was not the grateful face of the old beggar, but a terrible face from the past. Valjean thought he had seen the face of Javert.

The next night Valjean went again to see the old beggar. When Valjean gave him a few coins the old beggar raised his head and answered "Thank you kind Sir!" It was, indeed, only the old beggar.

Jean Valjean now felt silly. He even began to laugh. "To think that I thought I saw Javert. I must be getting old if my eyesight is that poor."

He walked home and tried to forget about the whole thing.

That night after he put Cosette to bed, he thought he heard footsteps on the stairs. He bent down to look through the keyhole, which was quite a large one, hoping to get a glimpse of the person who had just stopped outside his door.

He saw the figure of a man; tall, wearing a long coat, with a club under his arm. Valjean stood up in alarm. The man looked just like Javert.

Valjean listened through the door. He heard the man ask the landlady about who lived in each room and when they left and came home each day.

When the man was gone, Valjean went quickly to awake Cosette.

Valjean and Cosette were instantly in the street making as many turns as possible to be sure they weren't followed.

Cosette walked without asking any questions.

After suffering in silence for six years of her life she had learned to obey without asking why.

As eleven o'clock struck in the church tower, Valjean crossed the road in front of the Police Station under a large street lamp. He dashed across the street with Cosette and they hid in a dark alley, watching the police station.

One minute later, three men appeared. They were all tall, dressed in long dark coats, with round hats, and great clubs in their hands.

The men stopped in the middle of the street and talked, looking like they didn't know which way to go. Then another man came into the light, pointing directly into the alley where Valjean was hiding. As the man pointed, his face shone bright in the lamp light. It was indeed, Javert.

Valjean turned and ran with Cosette down the alley. Every door he tried was locked, every exit blocked. Javert now had him cornered. Valjean had walked right into a trap.

Valjean now saw at least eight men walking into the alley. Javert had apparently recruited more help at the police station.

These policemen, their clubs shining in the moonlight, were led by the tall form of Javert as they advanced slowly and with precaution. They checked every door, every crevice, every hiding place along the alley. They couldn't see Valjean yet, but soon it would all be over. He would go back to prison, and Cosette would be lost forever.

Valjean looked left, right, forward and back. There was only one direction left to go.

Up.

Thanks to his numerous escapes from the prison at Toulon, Valjean had become a master at climbing in the corner of a wall, with no ledges or handholds, as high as a sixth story.

Valjean looked around and saw the rope of an old broken lamp hanging in the alley. He walked over, cut it loose with his knife, and tied it around Cosette's waist.

"Father," she said, in a whisper, "I am afraid. Who is it that is coming?"

"Hush!" he said, thinking quickly, "it is Madam Thenardier. If you cry, if you make any noise, she will hear you and take you back."

Cosette became absolutely silent at once.

Valjean put the end of the rope in his teeth and wedged himself in the corner of the wall as he began to climb as quickly and as easily as if there had been a ladder. Just thirty seconds later he was kneeling on top of the wall at the end of the alley.

Cosette felt herself lifted suddenly into the air. Before she had time to think about what was happening, she was at the top of the wall and Valjean pulled her safely into his arms.

Jean Valjean looked down over the other side of the wall. He couldn't see anything in the darkness. He turned back toward the alley when he heard the thundering voice of Javert:

"Search the alleyway, find him now!"

The soldiers rushed into the alley below Valjean.

Jean Valjean picked up Cosette, looked hesitantly down into the darkness, and jumped.

Chapter 5: Payment for Heavy Lifting

Jean Valjean found himself in a sort of garden. As his eyes adjusted to the dim light he could make out a row of large poplar trees near him, and a large forbidding building towering above him.

He was about to put Cosette down when he heard a noise in the garden and he crouched down in fear. He listened, expecting Javert to appear at any moment, but what he heard was not forbidding, but inviting. A beautiful, almost heavenly sound was coming from the building nearby. It was a hymn being sung, he was hearing the pure sweet voices of women singing in church.

Valjean sat on the ground and listened to the sweet hymns being sung. He sat so long that Cosette fell asleep in his lap. Valjean eventually began to doze off as well, but sat up straight when he heard a little bell ringing in the garden.

Valjean could see a man walking towards him, a little bell ringing each time the man took a step. The man had a limp, and Valjean froze in terror as he realized this was likely one of the policeman who had jumped in after him, injuring his leg. He was ringing the bell to alert the other officers!

Valjean reached down to wake Cosette and felt that her hands were like ice.

He called to her in a low voice:

"Cosette!"

She did not open her eyes.

He shook her, she did not wake.

He frantically listened for her breathing; she was breathing; but slowly, and weakly. He was afraid she was freezing to death. How could he get her warm again?

He decided it was worth the risk, he had to get her warm, police or no police.

He walked straight to the man whom he saw limping in the garden.

"A hundred dollars for you if you will find me a fire to warm up my daughter, she is freezing."

The moon shone full in Jean Valjean's face as the man looked at him in shock.

"What, is it you, Mayor Madeleine?" Asked the man.

Valjean had almost forgotten that name, the one he had used for so many years.

He looked at the man speaking to him. It was an old man, bent over and lame, dressed much like a peasant, who had on his left knee a string with a bell hanging from it. The man took off his hat and said:

"How did you come here, Father Madeleine? How did you get in, did you fall from heaven?"

"Who are you? What is this house!" asked Jean Valjean. "And how do you know my name?"

"You saved my life," said the man.

The man turned, a ray of the moonlight lit up his face, and Jean Valjean recognized old Fosh.

Ah!" said Jean Valjean, "It is you? Yes, I remember you."

"And I certainly remember you!" said the old man.

Jean Valjean asked "What is this bell you have on your knee?"

"Oh that!" answered Fosh, "that is so that the nuns can hear me coming. They aren't supposed to see or talk to men, so when they hear the bell, they know I'm nearby, and they leave the area."

"Nuns?" asked Valjean

"Yes of course. Don't you remember? You got me the job here as the gardener. This is the Convent of the Petit Picpus."

Jean Valjean remembered. After old Fosh was crippled by his fall under the cart, Valjean the mayor had recommended him for a job at this convent in Paris.

Valjean continued: "Father Fosh, I once saved your life. Well, you can now return the favor."

"Oh! Sir Mayor, what can I do for you?

"First, help me get this poor child warm."

"Ah yes!" said Fosh, "the child!" He took them quickly to his small home in the garden.

In half an hour Cosette's face was rosy and warm before a good fire as she slept in the old gardener's bed. The two men were warming themselves, eating a simple dinner as Fosh told "Mayor Madeleine" all about the convent.

It was not just for nuns, but also a school for

young girls. Some stayed there and became nuns, others finished school and left the convent to live life out in the world. The convent was one of the oldest and finest in all of Paris. As Fosh gave more of its history, Valjean sat and thought.

Maybe we can stay here. Maybe Cosette can go to school here. No one would ever find us. No men can search in here, for no men are allowed other than the gardener. Besides, this would be a good life for her. She would learn of God, learn to serve him, and perhaps, dedicate her life to him.

"Could we stay here?" Valjean suddenly asked.

Fosh was taken aback.

"Here? Why would Sir the mayor wish to stay here? You are so strong, so smart, so needed by your city. I don't understand."

"I have resigned as mayor so that I can care for this child. I am now the only family she has. She needs a school, I need a job, and we both need a place to live."

"The Reverend mother would never agree to you living here. There are no men allowed except me. Well, she might consent if you were family."

"Then call me your brother," said Valjean. "Please, I need you to save my life as I saved yours."

So, the next morning, two little bells were heard tinkling in the garden. Jean Valjean was now known by everyone as Ultimus Fosh; the gardener's brother and the father of Cosette Fosh who had just been admitted to the school.

Part Three: Marius

Chapter 1: Colonel George Pontmercy

Sir Gillenormand was one of those crotchety old men who have far too much money and not nearly enough love.

He lived with his two adult daughters and his little grandson Marius. Marius was perfect in his grandfather's eyes. He ran and played and laughed and didn't have a care in the world. Grandfather Gillenormand doted on the young man, loving him with all the love he had felt for the boy's mother. She had always been Gillenormand's favorite. When she died in a tragic accident, her father thought she had only made one mistake in her entire life: marrying George Pontmercy.

George was a scoundrel in Sir Gillenormand's eyes. After all, the Gillernormands were an honorable family that honored and served their King. George was a traitor who had served as a Colonel in Emperor Napoleon's army. The only person that grandfather Gillenormand hated more than George Pontmercy, was Napoleon. Napoleon had destroyed France, destroyed the people, and had now destroyed Sir Gillenormand's family.

After Marius' mother died, Sir Gillenormand decided it was the perfect time to "fix things." He knew George was poor and couldn't possibly send Marius to a good school, give him a good home, or let him enjoy any of the riches of life, so he made George an offer:

Gillenormand said: "If you leave this house and never return, Marius will have everything he could ever want. I will send him to the best schools, give him the best things, and when I die, he will inherit everything. This only happens if you will leave him here, and never, ever, return."

George, much like Fantine, thought he was doing what was best for his child when he agreed to leave his child behind.

George only broke the agreement in secret, and then only every few months. He knew where Marius was taken to church, and every few months George would sneak in the back of the mass at Saint Sulpice and hide behind a pillar where he could watch his son without being noticed. Every time George saw his son he cried in silence behind the pillar, watching his boy a few feet away, knowing he would never talk to him.

After years of making these visits, the church-warden, Father Mabeuf, finally decided to speak to the man who he always saw hiding behind the pillar crying.

George Pontmercy told Father Mabeuf the whole story of what had happened to cause this strange situation. Father Mabeuf was touched by the story of this great but lonely father who was kept from his son by the wealth of the world.

In the year 1827, Marius had just turned eighteen

when his grandfather walked into his room with a letter in his hand.

"Marius," said Sir Gillenormand, "Your father died yesterday."

Marius had never even heard of his father. The news of his death didn't mean a thing. Marius had been told the story of what happened: once his mother had died his father had just left. Apparently, he didn't want a son. He had never come to see Marius in the last seventeen years. Why should Marius care about him now?

"So?" said Marius coldly.

"His funeral is tomorrow. You should go and pay your respects," said Gillenormand.

Marius shrugged and agreed to go.

Marius left late the next day and arrived in Vernon at sundown. He didn't see any reason to arrive on time. When he got to his father's home the funeral was almost over.

Marius wandered around the house waiting for the funeral to end. He noticed how poor and meager the house was. When he looked in the coffin and saw his father for the first time he felt nothing for him. To Marius – it was just a dead body. Marius turned and asked the woman in the room, "Did he leave me anything?

The woman handed him a scrap of paper.

It was written in the George's handwriting and said:

"For my Son: The Emperor made me a Baron upon the battlefield of Waterloo. Since King Louis XVIII refuses to recognize this title which I have bought with my blood, my son will take it and bear it. I need not say that he will be worthy of it."

On the back, the Colonel had written: "At this same battle of Waterloo, a sergeant saved my life. This man's name is Thenardier. I believe he runs a little inn in Montfermeil. If my son meets him, he will do Thenardier all the service he can."

Marius took this paper, folded it, and placed it in his pocket.

Marius stayed in Vernon only as long as he had to. After the burial, he returned to Paris and went back to his study of law.

On one day Marius had remembered he had a father, the next day he buried him, and the third day he forgot him.

Chapter 2: The Value of Going to Mass

Marius was now an adult. He was about to finish Law school and find his place in the world, yet he still kept some habits from his childhood, such as going to church. One Sunday he had gone to hear mass at Saint Sulpice, the same chapel where his aunt took him when he was a little boy. He wasn't really that interested in the sermon, so he sat behind a pillar paying no attention to the small engraved sign that read "Reserved for Father Mabeuf"

The mass had barely started when an old man tapped Marius on the shoulder and said: "Sir, this is my place."

Marius moved over and the old man took his seat.

After the mass, the old man turned to Marius and said: "I apologize for making you move, I know it must seem silly to reserve a seat in a church, especially behind a pillar."

"I didn't mind" interjected Marius.

"This seat has special meaning to me," continued the old man. "You see, for more than ten years, every two or three months, a poor, brave father came here because he had no other way of seeing his son. There had been some family disagreement banishing the father from the home. So, the father came here every few months and he watched his son in secret from this very seat. The little boy never suspected that his father was here. The father stayed hidden behind this pillar the whole time. I watched him, always looking at his child, and always weeping. The father died a few years ago, and his seat behind this pillar became sort of a sacred place to me. I now sit here every single mass and think of the love of that father. I met him once. I think his name was Pontmarie, Montpercy. Something like that. I wish I could remember."

"Pontmercy?" asked Marius, turning pale.

"Exactly; Pontmercy. Did you know him?"

"Sir," said Marius, "he was my father."

The old churchwarden clasped his hands, and exclaimed-

"You are the child! Well, you are certainly a man now! But you can say with more certainty than anyone that you had a father who loved you well."

Marius felt tears welling up in his eyes and Father Mabeuf stood to excuse himself as it was time for him to go home. Marius stood as well and offered his arm to the old man. Marius walked the old man home. They talked about George the whole way.

The next day Marius told his grandfather he would be gone for three days to go hunting. Sir Gillenormand knew Marius didn't like hunting, and figured he must running off after some young lady. "Take four days, go have fun!" he said.

Three days later Marius returned and went straight to the library of the law-school. He checked out all the records of war and searched and searched for any mention of his father.

Marius found a hospital note that said his father had suffered for a week with a high fever. Then he found a list of Generals under whom his father had served.

Marius went to visit each of these men, and every time Marius left the house his grandfather thought he was sneaking out to meet a new girlfriend.

Marius went to church at Saint Sulpice and talked for hours with the church-warden, Father Mabeuf told Marius all about his father's life in Vernon, how lonely, yet how noble he had been. Marius' love for his father grew and grew with each passing day.

Marius now regretted all the bad things he had ever said about his father. He wished he could hug him and hold him and tell him how much he loved him.

Marius also began to search for ways to honor his father. Colonel George Pontmercy had served Emperor Napoleon, while Sir Gillenormand served King Louis. Marius had grown up honoring the king, but no more. He would now be a staunch follower of Napoleon, and would do all he could to throw down the government of King Louis.

Marius became a revolutionary almost overnight. He read his father's last note again and decided he must wear the title his father had left for him. He went to an engraver in Paris and ordered a hundred cards bearing this name: "Barón Marius Pontmercy."

After taking his father's title, he now needed to honor his father's other wish: to give service to the man who saved his father's life: Thenardier.

Marius took another three-day trip, this time to Montfermeil to find the "Sergeant of Waterloo, the innkeeper Thenardier." When Marius arrived, the inn was closed. Thenardier's business had failed and nobody knew what had become of him.

Marius felt worthless and hopeless. He had insulted and belittled his father while he was alive. He had missed most of his father's funeral, and hadn't done more than glance at his father in the casket. Now he couldn't honor his father's last wish. He couldn't help this man, Thenardier.

Marius stopped in Vernon on his way home from Montfermeil and knelt before his father's grave. He swore, before God, his father, and all spirits in the cemetery; that he would find a way to prove his love for his father.

Marius returned home from Vernon early in the morning and was exhausted from spending two nights traveling. Feeling the need for a refreshing bath, he ran quickly up to his room, taking only enough time to take off his traveling coat and a black ribbon which he now wore around his neck.

Sir Gillenormand had heard him come in, and hurried as fast as he could with his old legs to climb to the top of the stairs where Marius' room was so he could give his grandson a hug and find out a little more about where he had been.

When Grandfather Gillenormand entered the room, Marius was already gone. The old man noticed the coat and the black ribbon.

A moment later Sir Gillenormand marched into his daughter's room with a big smile on his face. He held in one hand the coat and in the other the black ribbon, and cried:

"Victory! We are going to figure out the mystery!"

A small black box, much like a locket, was fastened to the ribbon.

"I'll bet there is a picture of some beautiful maiden inside this box. Marius has hung it from a ribbon so it can always be close to his heart. How romantic these young ones are!"

"Let us see, father."

The box opened by pressing a spring. They found nothing in it but a piece of paper carefully folded.

Sir Gillenormand burst out with laughter. "I know what this must be. A love-letter!"

"Ah! Then let us read it!" said the aunt as she put on her glasses. They unfolded the paper and read this:

"For my son: The Emperor made me a Baron upon the battlefield of Waterloo. Since King Louis XVIII refuses to recognize this title which I have bought with my blood, my son will take it and bear it. I need not say that he will be worthy of it."

The faces of both readers fell flat. They felt a cold chill run over them both. Sir Gillenormand said angrily:

"It is the handwriting of that bandit."

Just at that moment, a small package, wrapped in blue paper, fell from a pocket of Marius' coat. Mademoiselle Gillenormand picked it up and unfolded the wrapping paper. Inside were Marius' cards. She passed one of them to Sir Gillenormand, who read: Baron Marius Pontmercy.

The old man yelled for the housemaid. He took the ribbon, the box, and the coat, threw them all on the floor in a heap and said :

"Take away those things"

Grandfather Gillenormand and his daughter sat in silence until Marius came walking into the room. Marius saw his grandfather holding one of his cards. Marius opened his mouth to explain but his grandfather cut him off:

"Stop! Stop! Stop! Stop! Stop!" cried Gillenormand sarcastically. "You are a Baron now. Shall I kneel at your feet? Should I have the maid announce you when you walk into a room? What do these cards mean?"

Marius turned red and answered:

"They mean that I am my father's son."

Gillenormand's face turned hard as he said harshly:

"Your father? I am your father."

"My father," resumed Marius, "was a humble and heroic man who served the republic and France gloriously. He lived for 25 years in military camps, by day under bullets, by night in the snow, in the mud, in the rain. He fought battles, was wounded at least twenty times, and then he died forgotten and abandoned because he loved his son too much."

Sir Gillenormand's face had become red, then purple, then black with rage.

"Marius!" exclaimed he, "abominable child! Your father was a beggar, an assassin, a thief! Do you hear, Marius? Look at you, you are as much a baron as my slipper! All the followers of Napoleon were bandits! All of them traitors who betrayed their legitimate king! All cowards who ran from the English at Waterloo! That is what I know. Your father was a disgrace!"

Now it was Marius whose anger burned. He could not allow his father to be insulted like that. Marius was speechless. He didn't want to insult his grandfather who had raised him and loved him, but he could not forgive the old man for insulting his father. Marius decided he would not insult his grandfather, but instead, insult the thing he loved most.

Marius looked straight at his grandfather, and cried in a thundering voice:

"Down with the king, the great hog Louis XVIII!"

The old man's face suddenly turned white. He turned to his daughter and said:

"A baron like him and a gentleman like me cannot remain under the same roof."

Then Sir Gillenormand stood up and pointed to the door while glaring at Marius:

"Be off."

Marius ran out of the house and hailed a carriage. He had only the clothes he was wearing, his watch, and $30 in his wallet. He didn't know where he was going, or what he was doing. He only knew he had to get as far away from his grandfather as possible.

Chapter 3: Friends of the ABC

It was early afternoon and Coferac was leaning against the doorpost of his favorite cafe watching as the ladies walked by. He saw a carriage pass by, and a few minutes later, saw it pass by again, as if it were going in circles. When it drove by a third time he hailed the driver and the carriage stopped.

Coferac looked inside and saw a young man seated, staring at the wall of the carriage with a completely blank face.

"Where do you live?" asked Coferac.

"In this carriage," said the young man.

"Well aren't you rich?," replied Coferac. "With carriage rates you must pay $9000 a year in rent."

Just then Enjolras came out of the cafe.

The young man in the carriage smiled sadly: "I have been paying this rent for two hours, I just don't know quite where to go."

"What's your name?" asked Coferac.

"Marius... Baron Marius Pontmercy," replied the young man.

"Do you have you any political opinions, Sir Baron?" asked Enjolras, joining the conversation.

"What do you mean?" Asked Marius, almost offended at the question.

"Do you serve the King, or the Emperor?"

"I serve, well, I serve Emperor Napoleon," replied Marius.

"Perfect," said Enjolras as he grabbed Marius' bag out of the carriage. "Come with us."

Coferac and Enjolras escorted Marius through the cafe, through a back door, down a set of stairs, and finally into a large room with about fifteen other young men and a big red flag on the wall with the letters ABC painted on it.

Marius found himself in the meeting room of a group he didn't even know existed, "The Friends of the ABC."

They called themselves that because they were the friends of the common people, the oppressed, the "abased." In French the word for "abased" is abaisee, pronounced just like the letters A-B-C in French.

Most of the group were college students, a few had graduated and had real jobs. They were led by Enjolras, Comfehr, and Coferac.

Enjolras was an only son of rich parents. He was charming, handsome, and very formal, almost militant. He had deep green eyes and a high forehead and the strength and energy which only a 22-year-old can possess.

He focused his life entirely on politics and saving the people. He had never been attracted to a woman in his life. To him they were a useless distraction.

Enjolras represented the logic of the group, Comfehr represented its philosophy. Coferac was the middle man, the one who kept both men working together and kept the group moving towards a sensible, well planned revolution.

Marius was bewildered by this flock of young men about him. All of them started slapping him on the back, welcoming him, and asking him all sorts of political questions. He had only decided to follow Napoleon a week before, and he still had no idea what that even meant. He was just trying to honor his father.

Now he heard talk of philosophy, literature, art, history and religion; all in ways he had never imagined. He had been so sheltered by his grandfather that he had assumed there was nothing else, no other ideas, no other way of being or thinking.

He moved in with Coferac and studied law all day, and politics all night. For three years he studied until he finally passed his tests and became a lawyer. He sent a letter to his grandfather to tell him the news. The letter was not loving, but it was respectful. Sir Gillenormand took the letter with trembling hands, read it, and threw it, torn in pieces, into the fire. He mumbled to himself: "If you were not a fool, you would know that a man cannot be a baron and a lawyer at the same time."

Marius had lived in poverty for three years. Now that he was working as a lawyer he finally had enough money to rent his own apartment.

It was a wretched little room with no fireplace in a place called the Gorbeau building.

He could have afforded something nicer but he

was still spending all his extra money trying to find the man Thenardier. Marius still knew almost nothing other than his name. This name, Thenardier, was said with almost as much love and respect as his own father's name, George. Marius imagined this man as a brave sergeant who had carried his father to safety while being shot at with a thousand bullets at the battle of Waterloo.

Marius had learned at Montfermeil of the ruin and bankruptcy of the unlucky innkeeper. Yet nobody could give him any further news of Thenardier; everyone assumed he had moved overseas.

Marius didn't owe money to anyone, he hated debt. The only debt he had left was the one he felt hanging over his head, night and day; the one left him by his father, the debt to Thenardier.

Marius now even dreamt of the day he would repay this debt. He would meet Thenardier and say to him: "You do not know me, but I do know you. Here I am, I will do anything you ask!" This was his sweetest and most magnificent dream.

CHAPTER 4: LITTLE GAVROCHE

As Marius left his apartment one day, he noticed a little orphan boy knocking on the apartment door next to his.

"Do you need something to eat? Are you begging for money?" Marius asked the boy.

"Beg yourself!" the boy replied. "I'm here to check on me mum."

Marius looked at him surprised, and continued on his way to work.

The little boy was well dressed in men's pants, but he had not got them from his father. He also wore a woman's shirt, which was not from his mother. Strangers had clothed him in these rags out of charity. Still, he had a father and a mother. But his father never thought of him, and his mother did not love him. He was one of those children who have fathers and mothers, and yet they are orphans.

This little boy never felt so happy as when he was in the street. The cold pavement was softer and warmer than his mother's heart. His parents had thrown him out with a kick which he had decided was nothing more than a boost.

He was a boisterous, indignant little boy with a mouth to match his attitude.

He had no shelter, no food, no fire, no love, yet he was light-hearted because he was free. He usually slept in a big elephant statue down in the main square, but it had been about three months since he had seen his family, so he had walked to the most desolate and depraved part of Paris: the Gorbeau building.

Among those who lived in the building, the wretchedest of all were the boy's family: a father, mother, and two daughters nearly grown, all four lodging in the same room.

The family was completely destitute, and the father was a mystery. When the father had rented the room, he had said his name was Jondrette. A few days later he told the landlady that people might come looking for a man named Fabantou, or maybe Genflot, or even a Spaniard named Don Alvares or many other names. She was told to direct them all to his door, for he was an actor, and had played many famous roles for which he was remembered, and all these people would be searching for him.

This boy, coming home to his unloving parents, went by the name of little Gavroche. This time it took less than an hour for him to be kicked out again, back on the streets where he was as happy as could be.

That night when Marius returned home, he was smiling. He may have been living in a terrible apartment, but he was comfortable. He now liked to take long walks alone down the streets of Paris. He'd sometimes walk down through the Luxembourg or spend half a day looking at a vegetable garden.

That night he saw the landlady as he walked up to his apartment. She stopped him and told him that he may have new neighbors soon. The wretched Jondrette family were to be turned out into the street the very next morning. They were two months behind on their rent, and the landlady needed either the money, or the apartment.

"How much do they owe you total?" Marius asked.

"Twenty dollars," said the old woman.

Marius had thirty dollars in reserve in a drawer. He ran up to his room and came back down to the landlady.

"Here," he said to the old woman. "Here are twenty-five dollars. Pay the rent for those poor people, and then give them five dollars, and do not tell them that it is from me."

Chapter 5: Mr. White

Marius was now a fine-looking young man, of medium height, with heavy jet-black hair, a high intelligent brow, a frank and calm expression, and a smile that made shine in every moment. He was smart, charitable, thoughtful, and innocent.

Even when he had been the poorest and most depraved law-student, the girls had turned when he passed. He had always assumed they were looking at his old clothes; that they were laughing at him. The truth is, that they looked at him because of his graceful handsome appearance. Many girls dreamt about him for days.

A year later he still thought himself plain, poor, and undesirable. Marius took walks into all parts of Paris, meandering the streets, taking in the sights and sounds of the city he loved. He watched the people and saw some laughing, some crying, some loving, and others suffering.

One day, Marius decided to walk in a place he hadn't been in over a year, the Luxembourg.

As he walked he noticed a man across the way, seated on a stone bench with someone else seated beside him. The man looked to be about sixty years old. He seemed sad and serious. He looked like an old retired soldier. His expression was kind, but it did not invite conversation. He wore a blue coat and pants, and a broad-brimmed hat, and a fresh white handkerchief in his pocket. He looked like an old widower; his hair being perfectly white.

When Marius came near the man he heard a girl's voice and looked to see who was seated next to the man with white hair. Marius stopped suddenly. He stared in amazement at a noble, beautiful creature, with radiant chestnut hair highlighted with strands of gold; cheeks which seemed made of roses, skin of perfect whiteness, an exquisite mouth which had upon it a smile like a gleam of sunshine, and a voice like music.

Marius realized he was staring and he quickly resumed his walk and turned the next corner to hurry home. The girl had not seen him. As Marius looked at his clothes he was suddenly embarrassed. He had dared to walk in the Luxembourg in his filthy and unworthy "every day" suit while wearing a hat with a crease, and old scuffed boots.

The next day, Marius took from his closet a brand-new coat, new pants, a new hat, new freshly shined boots, as well as a pair of gloves. Then, and only then was he ready to go for a walk in the Luxembourg.

When Marius entered the walkway, he saw the man with white hair at the other end, seated in the same place. Marius had already named the old man "Mr. White," but no name seemed heavenly enough for the girl, so her name remained a mystery. Marius buttoned his coat, stretched it down to make sure there were no wrinkles, and marched toward them.

As he drew nearer, his steps became slower and slower. When he was still at least fifty steps away from their seat, he started sweating and he stopped completely. He was terrified. He quickly turned around and started walking home.

Then he stopped again, regained his courage, and turned around again, and marched directly passed her seat to the end of the walk. She hadn't noticed. He turned and passed again before the beautiful girl. This time he was very pale as his nervousness returned. Again, she didn't even look up once.

He walked home puzzled and confused, talking to himself. *"How could she not have noticed my shiny boots, my new pants, and perfectly pressed coat?"*

He was so worried that night that he forgot to go to dinner. He instead went home and planned out in meticulous detail, how he would get her attention the next day.

He did not go to sleep until he had carefully brushed and folded his coat.

The next day Marius dressed up the exact same way, and walked directly to the Luxembourg where he sat and watched the two from a distance. He could just make out the man's white hair, and her black hat. Marius sat there all day, and didn't go home until after dark.

The next day, he repeated the procedure. Two weeks passed this way. Every morning Marius put on his new suit and went to the Luxembourg to see her. On the last day of the second week, Marius was as usual sitting on his seat when suddenly he trembled. Something new was happening, something terrifying. Mr. White and his daughter had left their seat and they were coming slowly towards him. Marius closed his book, then he opened it again, then he made an attempt to read. He trembled. The most beautiful woman he had ever seen was walking straight towards him. *"O dear!"* thought he, *"I shall not have time to make a proper pose. Why are they coming so fast?"* he asked himself. He was overwhelmed. He heard their steps approaching. He sat in fear, bowed his head and waited. When they were quite near him he dared to look up. The young lady passed by, and as she did, she looked at him. She looked at him steadily, with a sweet and thoughtful look which made Marius tremble from head to foot. He felt as though his brain were on fire. She had come to him, what happiness! She now seemed more beautiful than she had ever seemed before.

One glance had done all that. It was all over for him. Marius now loved a woman.

Chapter 6: The Blunders of Love

A whole month passed during which Marius went every day to the Luxembourg. When the appointed hour came, nothing could possibly keep him away.

The girl had noticed him, and now she smiled at him each and every day. He stopped being cautious, and began walking by her more and more each day, sitting closer, walking slower, trying to always get her attention without letting Mr. White notice.

The young girl was much more subtle. She would continue her vocal conversation flawlessly with Mr. White, while having an entirely different conversation using her eyes with Marius.

After a month of this, Mr. White finally noticed the boy and became suspicious. Mr. White decided to test the young man, so when Marius came the next day Mr. White stood up and moved to the other end of the plaza. Mr. White wanted to see if Marius would follow them. Marius did not think anything of it and walked straight towards them.

After that day Mr. White began to change his habits. They didn't always arrive at the same time like they had. He didn't bring his daughter every day. Sometimes he came alone. When he was alone, he noticed that Marius did not stay. Another blunder.

Marius took no notice of these blunders. His love had made him blind, so he didn't see anything but her.

His love grew. He dreamed of her every night. One evening before leaving the Luxembourg, he found something more precious than he ever could have hoped for. He found, on the bench which Mr. White and his daughter had just left, a handkerchief. Marius grabbed it and examined it immediately. This handkerchief was embroidered with the letters U. F. Marius knew nothing of this beautiful girl, neither her family, nor her name, nor her address; these two letters were the first clue as to who she was. He was certain they were her initials.

"What name for an angel could start with a U?" he wondered.

"Ursula!" he thought. *"What a sweet name!"*

He kissed the handkerchief, inhaled its perfume, put it over his heart in the day-time, and at night went to sleep with it on his lips.

"I feel her whole soul in it!" he exclaimed.

In reality, this handkerchief belonged to the old gentleman, who had accidentally let it fall from his pocket. U.F. stood for Ultimus Fosh. That was the name the old man had taken, ever since becoming a gardener at the Convent at Petit Picpus. Mr. White was really Jean Valjean, and "Ursula", as Marius had named her, was Cosette. She had gone to school in the convent, and when her schooling was done, she had moved with Jean Valjean to a house nearby. Marius knew nothing of this. All he knew was that he had now had something that may have belonged to her; this precious, perfectly white handkerchief.

For days and days after finding it, Marius always appeared at the Luxembourg kissing this handkerchief and placing it on his heart. Cosette saw him do it, and was very confused. She had no idea what it was, or why he kept kissing it.

Marius thought he knew her name, now he wanted to know where she lived.

He had committed one blunder by following them when they switched seats. He had committed a second by not remaining at the Luxembourg when Mr. White came there alone. He next committed a third, a monstrous one. He followed "Ursula" to her home. It was a large three-story building with multiple tenants.

He knew her name; and he now knew where she lived. He next had to know who she was.

One night, after he had followed them home and seen them disappear into the house, he followed after them and said boldly to the doorman:

"The gentleman who just came in, he lives on the first floor, correct?"

"No," answered the doorman. "He lives on the third floor."

Marius smiled, another fact. This success made Marius bolder still.

"And what does this gentleman do?"

"He lives on his income, Sir. He's a very kind man, who does a great deal of good among the poor, even though he is not rich."

"What is his name?" continued Marius.

The doorman looked at Marius suspiciously and said "Are you a detective?"

Marius didn't know how to answer, so he turned and ran.

When he got home he was already smiling again. "Good," he thought. "I know that her name is Ursula, that she is the daughter of a retired gentleman, and that she lives there, on the third floor."

The next day Mr. White and his daughter made a very short visit to the Luxembourg, and when they quickly left, Marius followed them to their home.. On reaching the gate, Mr. White let his daughter go inside, and then stopped. Before entering himself, he turned and looked directly at Marius. Marius was so in love that he was oblivious to the meaning of the cold stare from Mr. White.

The next day they did not come to the Luxembourg. Marius waited in vain all day.

The day after, Marius waited all day again, and then went to their house to watch for a light from their windows.

A whole week went by this way. They never came to the Luxembourg again, and Marius now spent his nights staring at the third story windows, feeling his heart jump each time a shadow passed in front of a window.

On the eighth day when he reached their home, there was no light in the windows. "What!" he said, "What's wrong?" He waited till ten o'clock. Till midnight. Till one o'clock in the morning. No light appeared in the third story windows, and nobody entered the house. He went away very gloomy.

The next night he went again. No light in the windows; the blinds were closed; the third story was entirely dark.

Marius knocked at the gate and said to the doorman:

"What happened to the gentleman on the third floor?"

"Moved," answered the doorman.

Marius tottered, and said feebly: "Since when?"

"Yesterday."

"Where does he live now?"

"I don't know anything about it."

"He didn't leave his new address?"

"No," said the doorman. "Now move along."

Marius walked home in dejected despair.

CHAPTER 7: JONDRETTE

Summer passed, then autumn; winter came. Neither Mr. White nor the young girl had set foot in the Luxembourg ever again. Marius was dejected and had only one thought, to see that sweet adorable face again. He searched continually; he searched everywhere. He found nothing. He fell into a deep depression. It was all over now. Work disgusted him and walking now made him tired. It seemed to him that everything worth living for had disappeared.

He blamed himself a thousand times. "Why did I follow her? I was a fool. It is my fault."

Whenever he would see an older man with white hair, he would look twice, hoping it was Mr. White and he could follow him to Ursula – but it never was.

Marius still lived in the Gorbeau building. There were no other renters left but himself and those Jondrettes whose rent he had once paid. He had never spoken to them in all that time, not once.

Marius was just leaving for the night when he was bumped by two young girls running past him in rags, one tall and slender, the other a little shorter.

They fled past him and Marius noticed something at his feet. It was a package of letters.

"Those poor girls must have dropped this!"

He called after them but they had already vanished around the corner. He went inside his room and opened the package and found four letters.

All four letters were addressed to well known Parisians. All four used the same paper, stank like tobacco, and had the same handwriting; yet they had four different signatures.

One was signed "*Don Alveres*," the next "*Balizard,*" then "*Genflot*," and the last was signed "*Fabantou.*"

Marius put the letters back in the package, threw it into a corner, and went to bed.

The next morning, he awoke to a knock at his door. It was the eldest daughter of Jondrette. She was shivering in the cold as he noticed her raggedy clothing, dirty shoulder-blades and red hands. Her mouth hung open and appeared sunken with some teeth gone, her eyes were dull and drooping. She had the figure of a young girl, but the look of a corrupted old woman.

She stood in the doorway and held out her hand saying: "Here is a letter for you, Monsieur Marius."

How did she know his name? He was still trying to wake up and couldn't think clearly enough to figure it out.

He unfolded the letter and read:

My amiable neighbor, young man!

I have lerned of your kindness towards me, that you paid my rent six months ago. I bless you, young man. My eldest daughter will tell you that we have now been without a morsel of bread for two days, and my spouse is sick. If I am not desseived, I think you are a jenerus and kind man who will soften his heart and give us some small gift.

It was signed "Jondrette."

Suddenly everything became clear.

This letter came from the same source as the other four. It was the same writing, the same style, the same paper, the same stench of tobacco. The ;letter was also terribly misspelled.

Marius understood now what his neighbor did each day. Jondrette was a con man who convinced rich people to pay his rent and give him gifts. He lived off the generosity of others by deceiving them. Marius' thoughts were suddenly interrupted by the Jondrette girl:

"Do you know, Monsieur Marius, that you are a very pretty boy?"

This made her smile and made him blush.

She walked over to him, and laid her hand on his shoulder: "You pay no attention to me, but I know you, Monsieur Marius. I meet you here on the stairs, and then I see you visiting Father Mabeuf at the church when I follow you that way. I like your tangled hair."

Her voice tried to be soft and lovely, but came out low and gravely, like a man's.

Marius stepped away from her.

"Mademoiselle," he said, "I have here a packet, which is yours, I think" and he handed her the package, which contained the four letters.

She clapped her hands and exclaimed:

"You have found it! We have looked everywhere! You see, this dropped when we ran. It was my brat of a sister who made the stupid blunder. When we got home, we could not find it. As we did not want to be beaten, we said that we had carried the letters to the persons, and that they had refused to help us.

This reminded Marius of what the poor girl had come to his room for.

He felt in his pocket and found five dollars and sixteen cents. This was, at the time, all the money that he had in the world. He kept the sixteen cents so he could buy dinner that night, and gave the five dollars to the young girl.

She took the money eagerly, and made a low bow to Marius, then waved her hand saying:

"Good day Sir. I am going to find my old man."

CHAPTER 8: LES MISÉRABLES

For five years Marius had lived in poverty, in privation, in distress even, but he realized that he had never known real misery. Real misery he had just seen. It was this poor creature which had just passed before his eyes. Nothing but a thin wall separated him from this family who lived by begging, and he had never really noticed them.

They were the saddest and most terrible kind of people. They were depraved, corrupt, vile, hateful; in fact, their existence can only be described in one way. They were Les Misérables, the miserable ones.

Marius thought of this poor family and wondered what more he should have done for them. He had paid their rent and given them $5 six months ago, now he had given them $5 more.

Just then he heard someone yelling next door: "He is coming!"

Marius looked at the thin wall between their apartments and saw the cracks in plaster wall. Then he noticed that way up high, above his dresser, there was a hole in the wall where the plaster had fallen out completely. Marius climbed up on top of his dresser and peered into the hole, he could see the entire Jondrette apartment.

"Who is coming?" Marius heard Jondrette ask.

"The old man, from church!" said the eldest daughter.

Marius now watched as the conversation continued:

"You are sure?" asked Jondrette

"I am sure. He is coming in a carriage."

"In a carriage. Is he a Rothschild? Never mind. Wife, lie on the pallet, and do your best to look sick. 'Ponine, break a pane of glass in the window. Do it now!"

His eldest daughter punched the glass, breaking it. She also cut her hand and began crying as the cold winter air came blowing into the room through the broken window

"Perfect," said Jondrette. Now we are ready to receive him."

There was a light knock at the door and Jondrette rushed forward and opened it, bowing repeatedly and saying:

"Come in Sir, as well as your charming young lady."

An old man and a young girl appeared at the doorway.

Marius froze as he peered through the hole in the wall. What he felt at that moment escapes human language.

It was She.

Whoever has loved knows the deep meaning of that word: She.

Marius saw that sweet girl, that star which had been his light, that beautiful face which had vanished six months before.

She appeared now in this den of thieves and cons, together with Mr. White.

She stepped into the room with Mr. White and laid a large package on the table.

Mr. White approached with his kind and compassionate look, and said to the father:

"Sir Fabantou, you will find in this package some new clothes, some socks, and some new bedding."

"Our generous nobleman overwhelms us," said Jondrette. "But look sir. We also have no bread, no fire. A broken window! In such weather as is this! My spouse in bed! sick!"

"Poor woman!" said Mr. White as he saw her give a fake cough.

"My daughter injured!" added Jondrette as he secretly pinched 'Ponine's injured hand.

She cried out loudly in real pain.

"Her bleeding wrist!" said Jondrette, "It is an accident which happened working in a factory where she earned six cents a day. It may be necessary to cut off her arm."

"Really?" asked the old gentleman alarmed.

The girl, taking this seriously, began to sob again even louder.

"Alas, yes, my noble philanthropist!" answered the father.

For some time Jondrette had been looking at the philanthropist in a strange manner. He looked at him closely as if he were trying to recall some long-lost memory.

"Tomorrow is the 4th of February" continued Jondrette. "The last day I can pay my landlord. Tomorrow my injured daughter, myself, my spouse with her fever, my little girl, we shall all four be kicked into the street to freeze in the snow. You see, sir, I am behind on rent by an entire year! That is sixty dollars."

Maruis knew Jondrette was lying. He could not have owed for an entire year. It had only been six months since Marius had paid for two.

Mr. White took five dollars from his pocket and placed them on the table.

"Sir Fabantou," he said, "I have only these five dollars with me; but I am going to take my daughter home, and I will return this very evening since your rent is due tonight. Is that correct?

Jondrette's face lit up with a strange expression. He answered quickly:

"Yes, my noble Sir. At eight o'clock, I must be at my landlord's."

"I will be here at six o'clock, and I will bring you the sixty dollars."

"Mmm-hmm" mumbled Jondrette, distractedly.

"Till this evening then" said Mr. White.

"Six o'clock," said Jondrette.

Marius had only one thought, to follow her. He had lost her once before, he would not lose her again.

He leaped down from the dresser and took his hat. He ran to the stairs and hurried down to the street in time to see a carriage turn the corner.

Marius ran after her but knew he would never

catch up.

Marius saw a public cab passing by and he yelled out for it to stop.

The driver stopped, looked at Marius, and reached his left hand out rubbing his thumb and forefinger together.

"What?" said Marius.

"Pay in advance," said the driver, having noticed Marius' torn clothing.

"How much?" asked Marius as he remembered that he had only sixteen cents with him.

"Forty cents."

"I will pay when I get back."

The driver made no reply, but whistled loudly and snapped the reigns.

Marius saw the cab hurry away. Because of twenty-four cents he was losing his joy, his happiness, his love!

He thought bitterly of the five dollars he had given that very morning to that miserable girl from that terrible family. If he had those five dollars he could have found his love.

He returned home in despair. He went into his room and pushed his door closed behind him.

It did not close. He turned and saw a hand holding the door partly open.

"What is it?" he asked; "who is there?"

It was the Jondrette girl.

"You again?" said Marius harshly. "What do you want from me?"

"Sir Marius, you look sad. What is the matter with you?"

"There is nothing the matter with me."

"I tell you there is!" she insisted.

An idea came into Marius' mind.

"Listen," he said to her kindly.

"Oh! yes, talk softly to me! I like that better."

Marius continued: "Well, you had an old man and his daughter at your place tonight, right?"

"Yes."

"Do you know their address?"

"No."

"I want you to find it for me."

The girl's eyes, which had been gloomy, had become joyful.

"That's all you want, his address?"

Then she thought for a moment and added: "You mean you want HER address."

"Yes, can you do it?" said Marius.

"You shall have the beautiful young lady's address. But what will you give me?"

"Anything you wish!"

"Anything I wish?"

"Yes."

"Very well," she said. "you shall have the address."

She quickly ran out the door.

Marius dropped into a chair, with his head and both elbows on the table. So much had taken place since morning, the appearance of his angel, her disappearance, and now a glimmer of hope again. He was so overwhelmed he fell asleep.

Chapter 9: Setting the Trap

Suddenly Marius was violently awakened from his sleep.

He heard the loud, harsh voice of Jondrette:

"I tell you that I am sure of it, I recognized him!"

Marius leapt up onto the dresser again, hoping to hear something about his love.

He peered through the hole into the Jondrette den.

Jondrette was walking back and forth with rapid strides.

His wife asked: "What, really? you are sure?"

"Sure! It was eight years ago, but I recognize him! Ah! I recognize him! He is the same height, the same face, hardly any older. He is better dressed, that is all! Ah! Mysterious old devil, I have got you, all right! And the young lady-"

"Well, what about her?" said the woman.

Marius listened closely to hear what he could about his love, but just then Jondrette stooped down, and whispered in his wife's ear.

"That girl?" said the wife.

"That girl!" said the husband.

"Impossible!" she exclaimed, "When I think that my daughters go barefoot, wearing rags and she walks in here wearing a satin dress and a velvet hat! My blood boils!"

"My fortune is made," Jondrette mumbled to

himself.

"How?" asked the woman.

"I'll get my crew. He will come this evening at six o'clock. Our neighbor will be at dinner then and the landlady will be washing dishes in the city. The house will be empty. Our nobleman will either give us his fortune, or his life." Jondrette burst into a terrible laugh.

It was the first time that Marius had seen him laugh. This laugh was cold and sinister and made Marius shudder.

"Now," said Jondrette to his wife, "I am going out. I have some men to see. I shall be back as soon as possible."

Jondrette closed the door, and Marius heard his steps recede along the hall and go rapidly down the stairs. Just then the clock of the church struck one.

Marius got down from the dresser as quietly as he could. He put on his nice coat, took his hat, and went out, walking quickly to the nearest police station.

The office boy told Marius that the police chief was not in, but there was an inspector available.

As Marius walked into the Inspector's office he was taken aback by him. A man of tall stature was standing there behind a railing. He had a square face, a thin and firm mouth, very fierce, bushy grayish whiskers, and an eye that would turn your pockets inside out. This man's appearance was not much less ferocious or formidable than Jondrette's.

"What do you want?" he asked Marius.

Marius related his adventure: That a man was to be ambushed that very evening. That Marius had heard the whole plot through the hole in the wall; that the scoundrel who had contrived the plot was named Jondrette. The ambush was scheduled for tonight at six o'clock, in the Gorbeau building numbered 50-52.

"No. 50-52" said the Inspector. "I know the shanty. Impossible to hide ourselves inside without the thieves seeing us."

He turned towards Marius and asked: "Will you be afraid?"

"No more than you!" replied Marius rudely.

The inspector looked at Marius and plunged both his hands, which were enormous, into the pockets of his overcoat, and took out two small pistols. He gave the guns to Marius, saying:

"Take these. Go back home. Hide yourself in your room; let them think you have gone out. They are already loaded. You will watch through the hole in the wall you mentioned. When the generous man arrives, let them talk a little. When you see that the old man is in danger, fire off a pistol shot. I'll take care of the rest."

Marius took the guns and put them in the side pocket of his coat. As he opened the door to go, the inspector called to him: "If you need me between now and then, ask for Inspector Javert."

Marius sat down on his bed. It was 5:30 when Marius heard Jondrette come in next door.

"Have you greased the hinges of the door, so that

they shall not make any noise?"

"Yes," answered his wife.

"What time is it?"

"Almost six o'clock."

"The devil!" said Jondrette, "has the landlady gone out?"

"Yes," said the wife.

"Are you sure there is nobody at home in our neighbor's room?"

"He has not been back to-day, and you know that it is his dinner time."

"All right then girls, to your posts!"

"We have to stand barefoot in the snow?!" they protested.

"Don't worry about that, tomorrow you shall have boots of silk!" said the father.

They scurried out the door to take their places.

Marius grasped the pistol which was in his right pocket, took it out, and cocked it back, ready to fire.

The pistol in cocking gave a little clear, sharp click.

Jondrette heard the click and half rose from his chair.

"Who is there?" he called out.

Marius held his breath; Jondrette listened for a moment, then began to laugh, saying-

"What a fool I am? It is the wall, cracking like always."

Marius kept holding his breath with the pistol in his hand.

Chapter 10: Hesitation

At six o'clock sharp there was a knock at the door.

"Come in," said Mrs. Jondrette.

"Come in, Sir," repeated Jondrette, standing quickly.

Mr. White walked in and placed $80 upon the table.

"Sir Fabantou," he said, "that is for your rent and your pressing needs. Now let's talk about the rest."

"God reward you, my generous nobleman!" said Jondrette.

As Jondrette continued to praise and to adore Mr. White, Marius sat with horror, but no fear. He held the cocked pistol and felt reassured. "I shall stop this wretch when I please," he thought.

He knew the police were somewhere nearby, awaiting the signal of his gun to show their force and save Mr. White, the father of the girl he loved.

"Madam Fabantou, is she, all right?" asked Mr. White as he saw her slip between him and the door, as if she were guarding the exit.

"She is dying," said Jondrette. "But you see, Sir! She has so much courage, that woman! She is strong like an ox, no fear in her."

The woman, touched by the compliment, gave a smirk:

"You are always too kind to me, Sir Jondrette."

"Jondrette?" asked Mr. White, "I thought that

your name was Fabantou."

"Fabantou or Jondrette!" replied the husband hastily. "Who can recall? That is the way of an artist! Ha-Haa!"

While Jondrette was talking, Marius saw at the back of the room somebody who he hadn't seen before. A man had come in so noiselessly that nobody had heard the door turn on its hinges. This man's arms were bare and tattooed, his face stained black. He sat down in silence on the nearest bed behind the woman.

"Who is that man?" asked Mr. White who was watching everything and noticed everything.

"That man?" said Jondrette, "that is a neighbor. Pay no attention to him. I was about to tell you my dear patron, that I have a picture to sell."

A slight noise was made at the door. A second man entered, and sat down on the bed as well. He had his arms bare, like the first, and a mask of soot.

Mr. White stared at the man as Jondrette said: "Do not mind them. They are people of the house. I was telling you, then, that I have a valuable painting. Here, Sir, look."

"What is it?" asked Mr. White.

Jondrette exclaimed: "A painting by a master; a picture of great price. I cherish it like my own daughters, yet I am so unfortunate that I would part with it."

Mr. White glanced towards the back of the room. There were now four men; all four bare-armed, motionless, and with blackened faces.

"But this is some old inn sign, it is worth about three dollars," said Mr. White.

Jondrette answered calmly:

"Have you your pocket-book here? I will be satisfied with a thousand dollars."

Mr. White rose to his feet in fear as Jondrette came right up in his face: "But all this is not the real question! Do you know me?"

"No," insisted Mr. White.

Jondrette leaned forward over the candle and pushing his ferocious jaws up towards the calm face of Mr. White as he said emphatically:

"My name is not Fabantou, my name is not Jondrette, my name is Thenardier! I am the innkeeper of Montfermeil. I am the man you robbed when you took that little Lark! Now do you know me?"

An imperceptible flush passed over Mr. White's face yet he answered calmly and flatly:

"No more than before."

Marius had suddenly felt himself become frozen in place. The gun in his hand could no longer be fired. When Jondrette had said: "My name is Thenardier," Marius had trembled in every limb. He felt as if a sword had stabbed him in the heart. Then his right arm, which was just ready to fire the signal shot, dropped slowly down.

"Thenardier" was the name Marius knew by heart. This was the name written in his father's will! Marius carried this name in the holiest spot of his memory.

His father had written: "A man named Thenardier saved my life. If my son should meet him, he will do him all the good he can."

Here was Thenardier, that innkeeper of Montfermeil, for whom Marius had so long and so vainly searched!

Marius had found him at last, and this savior of his father was a bandit! This man, to whom Marius had sworn to devote himself, was a monster!

If Marius fired the gun, Mr. White would be saved and Thenardier imprisoned; if Marius did not fire, Mr. White would be beaten and robbed and Thenardier would escape. What was to be done? Which should he choose?

He seemed on the one hand to hear his love, "his Ursula" begging him to save her father, and on the other hand Marius heard his father pleading with him to save Thenardier. Marius shuddered as he felt that he was about to crack under the mental pressure.

CHAPTER 11: ALWAYS DETAIN THE VICTIM FIRST

"Ha!" cried Thenardier, "I have found you again at last, Sir threadbare millionaire! Sir giver of dolls! What a fake! What a charlatan you child-stealer!"

"I do not know what you mean" said Mr. White. "You are mistaken. I am a very poor man and anything but a millionaire. I do not know you; you mistake me for another."

"Ha!" screamed Thenardier, "You stick to that lie. I'll get the millions you owe me, and I'll get them tonight.

Mr. White rapidly pushed the chair away with his foot, the table with his hand, and with amazing speed he sprang to the window. Six strong hands seized him and drew him forcibly back into the room. Three of the black faced men had thrown themselves upon him.

"Search him!" cried Thenardier. "Take everything he's got."

Marius was once again tormenting the trigger of his pistol. He was in despair and could not decide what to do. Suddenly he didn't have to.

Everyone heard a great set of footsteps at the door and turned around. It was Javert. He had his hat in his hand, and he was just standing there, smiling.

Javert had waited outside long enough and had finally decided to go up without waiting for the pistol shot.

The frightened bandits rushed for their weapons as Javert calmly put on his hat and stepped into the room, his arms folded, his cane under his arm, his sword in its sheath.

"Halt there," he said. "You will not escape. There are seven of you, fifteen of us. Don't make us chase you, come quietly."

One of the bandits whispered in Thenardier's ear:

"It is Javert. I dare not fire at that man. Dare you?"

Thenardier took the pistol from the man and aimed at Javert.

Javert, who was within three paces, looked at him steadily and said:

"Don't fire, now! It will flash in the pan."

Thenardier pulled the trigger. The pistol flashed in the pan, burning Thenardier's hand.

"I told you so!" said Javert.

One of the bandits slid his tomahawk across the floor to Javert's feet.

"You are the emperor of the devils! I surrender."

"And you?" asked Javert of the other bandits.

They answered:

"We, too."

Javert replied calmly: "Very well."

"Handcuffs on all!" cried Javert over his shoulder.

Fifteen police officers entered and quickly handcuffed the four bandits, Thenardier, and his wife.

Just then Javert remembered the prisoner of the

bandits, who, since the entrance of the police, had not uttered a word, and had held his head down.

"Untie the prisoner and sit him here!" said Javert.

This said, he sat down with authority at the table, drew a stamped sheet from his pocket, and prepared for his interrogation.

When he had written the first lines he raised his eyes:

"I said bring forward the gentleman whom these thieves had bound."

The officers looked around.

"Well," asked Javert, "where is he?"

The prisoner of the bandits, Mr. White, had disappeared.

The door was guarded, but the window was not. As soon as he saw that he was unbound, and while Javert was writing, he had taken advantage of the confusion. In a moment when their attention was on the bandits, ValJean had leapt out of the window.

An officer ran to the window, and looked out; nobody could be seen outside.

"The devil!" said Javert, between his teeth, "that must have been the best one."

Part Four: Eponine

CHAPTER 1: EPONINE SUCCEEDS

It had been three months since Marius had watched Mr. White escape from Thenardier's men by jumping out the window.

Marius had moved out the next day and gone to live with Coferac. Even after seeing what a terrible man Thenardier was, Marius still felt a duty to help him. So every Monday, Marius sent five dollars to Thenardier in prison.

For Marius, everything was once again in darkness. He had felt a moment of hope; he had seen his love, his angel, for a moment. Now she was gone forever.

The days passed, one after another, and there was never anything new.

Marius now visited nobody except Father Mabeuf at church.

One day while he was at church, just after the service had ended, he heard a voice say: "Ah! there he is!" He looked over and saw Father Mabeuf pointing him out to a girl in the church doorway.

Marius recognized her immediately. It was the oldest of the Thenardier girls; the one called Eponine.

She looked terrible. She was barefooted and dressed in rags. Now her rags were three months older; the holes were larger, the tatters dirtier. She still had the same rough voice as she said to him: "I found you at last Sir Marius. Do you know I spent twenty days in jail? Oh! How I have looked for you! It's been weeks, now. When you moved away, it was very hard to find you."

"I'm sorry, I had to get away from that place." He replied

"You don't seem to be glad to see me?"

Marius thought of her father, of that night, and how he had lost the girl he loved. He said nothing.

"But if I would," she continued. "I could easily make you glad!"

"How?" inquired Marius. "What do you mean?"

She bit her lip; she seemed to hesitate, as if passing through a kind of interior struggle. At last, she nodded her head.

"You look sad, I want you to be glad. But promise me that you will laugh, and remember, you promised me that you would give me whatever I should ask-"

"What?" Marius asked, not understanding anything.

"I have the address of the young lady."

Marius smiled as he took her hand and almost yelled in excitement.

"Oh! Come! Tell me! Ask me for whatever you will! I'll give anything!"

"Come with me," she answered, walking him out of the church. "I am not sure of the street and the number; but I know the house well. I will show you."

A cloud passed over Marius' brow. He seized Eponine by the arm:

"Swear to me one thing!"

"Swear?" she asked, "swear what?"

"Your father!" he said. "Promise me, Eponine! Swear to me that you will not give her address to your father!"

She turned towards him with an astounded appearance.

"That is nice! you called me Eponine!"

Marius now caught her by both arms at once.

"But answer me now, in heaven's name! Swear to me that you will not give the address you know to your father!"

"My father?" she said. "Oh! yes. my father! Don' worry about him. He's still in prison."

"But you don't promise me!" exclaimed Marius.

"Yes! yes! I promise you that! I swear to you that!"

"Nor to anybody?" asked Marius.

"Nor to anybody."

"Now," added Marius, "show me the way."

"Come," she said, as they walked toward Plumet street.

Chapter 2: The House on Plumet Street

On Plumet Street there was a two-story house with a garden and a large iron gate which opened onto the street. This was all that could be seen from the street; but in the rear of the house there was a small yard, and at the back of it there was a second building, much smaller than the house.

In October, 1829, Valjean had moved in, bringing Cosette and an elderly maid, Tousant, with them. The neighbors did not gossip about it, because there were no neighbors. That was part of the reason Valjean liked the house so much.

Why had he left the convent? Jean Valjean had been happy there, so happy that his conscience at last began to be troubled. His life had been too perfect. He saw Cosette every day and nothing could take her from him. It seemed it would always be that way. She would become a nun and the convent would forever be their home. Then he started having doubts. Was he taking advantage of Cosette? Was he stealing her happiness to make his own? Was this a form of robbery, stealing a life from her she would never know was possible? He had realized that she deserved to know what normal life was like before giving it up to become a nun.

He resolved to leave the convent.

The only possession he took with him when he

left the convent was a little box. This box puzzled Cosette. Valjean always had it in his room and it was the only thing he always kept safe. Cosette laughed about it and called this box "the inseparable." She even told him: "I am jealous of that box."

Valjean brought his "inseparable" to the house near the Luxembourg where Marius had followed them. Now he had moved again, bringing the inseparable with them to a new house in Plumet street. While Cosette occasionally left the house, Valjean closed himself off even further from the world. He was so cautious that he rented two other homes in Paris so they would always have an instant escape if they were found.

He didn't want another disaster like had happened at their home near the Luxembourg.

When they had left the convent, Cosette could not have found a happier home. She had moved there when still a child and Jean Valjean had given her a small garden. "Do whatever you like with it," he had told her. It delighted Cosette; she searched through every inch and turned over every stone, she chased little animals during the day and dreamed about them at night. She loved that garden and her father, Jean Valjean, with all her heart.

Cosette had but only a vague memory of her early childhood. The Thenardiers haunted her nightmares, but she always remembered that Jean Valjean had saved her from them. She knew him as her father, and she had almost no memory of her mother, though

Valjean told her to pray for her mother every morning and evening.

Cosette did not even know her name. Whenever she asked Jean Valjean what her mother's name was, he stayed silent. If she repeated her question, he smiled at her as he shed a tear.

One day, years after moving from the convent, Cosette happened to look in her mirror and shocked herself. For the first time she noticed that she was pretty. This threw her into a strange anxiety. She had never even thought about being pretty.

Three months later she was truly beautiful. Her form was complete, her skin had become white, her hair had grown lustrous; there was even a new light in her blue eyes.

This scared Valjean. If he had noticed she was beautiful, that meant boys had figured it out as well. Valjean started watching her closer and noted that she had changed the style of clothes she wore. In less than a month she went from dressing shabbily to being one of the best dressed girls in all of Paris.

Valjean also noticed that Cosette, who previously was always asking to stay in, was now always asking to go out. What is the use, she thought, of having a pretty face and a delightful dress, if you do not show them to people?

It was at that time that Marius had seen her at the Luxembourg. He had fallen for her, followed her, and then scared her father into running away.

They had moved near the Luxembourg when they

left the convent, then they had moved to Plumet Street when Valjean noticed Marius following them.

Cosette did not complain. She asked no questions, she did not seek to know any reason. She was so depressed from losing Marius that she lost the strength to even resist. Valjean noticed that she had become sad and a few months later he thought he'd test the water and see if a trip back to the Luxembourg would please her.

He asked Cosette:

"Would you like to go to the Luxembourg?"

A light illuminated Cosette's pale face.

"Yes," she said excitedly.

They went, but three months had passed and Marius had stopped coming.

The next day, Jean Valjean asked Cosette again:

"Would you like to go to the Luxembourg?"

"No," she answered sadly and quietly.

Their lives grew darker and darker with only one light left. They still carried bread to those who were hungry, and clothing to those who were cold. In these visits to the poor, they still enjoyed life. They felt joy in helping others and even laughed together on their travels. Life continued this way until they had offered to help a poor family which turned out to be the Thenardiers. After Valjean's narrow escape he had retreated back to a secret, isolated life. When spring came he wouldn't even let Cosette leave their property. She could walk in the garden, but that was as far as she could go.

Walking in the garden made her happy. Eventually Valjean felt a little safe and he resumed his solitary walks at night. Both of them gradually became more lighthearted, more calm, more joyous, and more careless.

Chapter 3: A Letter Shines Bright

One evening in this same month of April, Jean Valjean had gone out. After sunset Cosette had sat down on her customary stone bench near the grated gate in the garden.

Cosette got up and meandered around the garden, walking in the grass which was wet with dew, until finally she was back at her seat. As she sat down she noticed on the bench a very large stone which had not been there a moment before.

She nervously lifted the stone and found underneath a white paper envelope. Cosette seized it; there was no address.

Cosette looked for a name, there was none; a signature, there was none. Who was it for? Who was it from? An irresistible fascination took possession of her. She couldn't turn her eyes away from this letter even for a second. She opened it and began to read. As she read it she gradually fell into ecstasy. After half an hour she finally raised her eyes from the last line of the last page and she turned instantly back to the beginning to read it again.

It was written in perfect hand-writing, thought Cosette. She could tell from the light and dark ink that it had been written over many different days. Cosette had never read anything like it. This fifteen-page letter opened her eyes to the true meaning of love. She felt in these pages a passionate, generous, honest nature; a boundless hope.

What was this letter with no address, no name, no date, no signature? Mystery surrounded this treasure. Whom could it come from? Who could have written these pages?

Cosette did not hesitate for a moment. She knew. One single man.

He!

All at once, she had the feeling somebody was standing behind her. She turned her head and arose.

It was he.

Cosette, ready to faint, did not utter a sound. She drew back slowly as she felt herself attracted forward.

Then she heard his voice: "Pardon me for intruding, I am here because my heart is bursting, I could not live as I was, so I had to find you. Have you read the letter I placed on this seat? Do you recognize me at all? Do you remember the day when you looked upon me? It was at the Luxembourg. I followed you to your house, but then you disappeared. I searched for you everywhere. When I found out you lived here I started coming here at night, just to see the light in your window and to think of you. Once I heard you sing. It made me so happy. I'm sorry if that worries you or scares you. You see, you are my angel, I don't think I could live without you."

"O my!" she said as she began to the fall onto the bench as if she were fainting.

He caught her as she fell. He held her in his

arms, he grasped her tightly. She then reached down and took his hand and laid it on her heart. He felt the paper there, and stammered:
"My letter? You love me, then?"

She answered in a voice so quiet that it could scarcely be heard:

"Of course! You know it!"

She then laid her blushing head on the chest of this proud and intoxicated young man.

He sat down on the bench by her side. There were no more words. One kiss was shared and that was all. Both trembled, and they looked at each other in the darkness with brilliant eyes.

They felt neither the fresh night, nor the cold stone, nor the damp ground, nor the wet grass. They looked at each other and their hearts were full. They had clasped hands, without knowing it. Gradually they began to talk. The night was serene and splendid above their heads. These two pure beings told each other all their dreams, their fears, their hopes, their ecstasies, how they had adored each other from afar, how they had longed for each other, and their despair when they thought they had lost each other. These two hearts poured themselves out into each other, so that at the end of an hour, it was the young man who had the young girl's soul and the young girl who had the soul of the young man.

When they had finished; when they had told each other everything; she laid her head upon his shoulder, and asked him:

"What is your name?"

"My name is Marius," he said. "And yours?"

"I'm Cosette."

Chapter 4: Conspirators Abound

That same night, an escape had occurred at the prison. Thenardier and his crew had been conspiring for months, and that night their plans were executed. With the help of little Gavroche, all the imprisoned men escaped into the sewers of Paris.

The first person Thenardier looked for when he was free was Eponine. She had always been a good scout, looking for rich folks to con or houses to rob.

Eponine had indeed scouted out a house recently. It wasn't for her father but rather for Marius. She had been willing to do anything for the boy she adored, even if it meant helping him fall in love with someone else.

Now, every night in that garden, Marius and Cosette clasped each other's hands as they walked and talked. Their first kiss was their only kiss. Marius had since only held Cosette's hand. She refused nothing and he asked nothing. It was pure love.

Jean Valjean still suspected nothing and Cosette was careful to never give any reason for suspicion.

Did he wish to take a walk?

"Yes, my dear father."

Did he wish to remain at home?

"Very well."

Would he spend the evening with Cosette?

She couldn't be happier.

As he always retired at ten o'clock, Marius often waited to come to the garden till after that hour.

Marius never went in the house. When he was with Cosette they hid themselves in a corner of the garden where they couldn't be seen or heard from the street. They sat there, holding hands and talking for hours.

Marius came in and out of the garden by removing a loose bar in the grated gate and replacing it so no difference could be seen. He often didn't leave until after midnight to sleep at Coferac's place.

"Would you believe it?" Coferac said one day to his friend Enjolras. "Marius comes home nowadays at one o'clock in the morning."

Coferac, a practical man, was not happy about Marius' new found love. Marius was starting to forget the important things in life.

One morning, Coferac confronted him:

"Come now my dear boy, tell us all her name. Confess thy love."

They prodded and plead, but nothing could make Marius "confess." He would tell no one her name. You might have torn his toe nails off before he would say the two sacred syllables of her name: "Cosette."

To Marius, this was a symbol of true love. To Coferac, this was betrayal.

Marius was careless and carefree. He stopped worrying and stopped paying attention to anyone other than Cosette. One evening as he made his way to her home, he was just turning the corner of Plumet Street, when he heard someone say:

"Good evening, Sir Marius."

He looked up, and recognized Eponine. He had not thought even once of this girl since the day she brought him to Plumet Street. She had completely gone out of his mind. He owed everything to her for finding Cosette's house, yet he still felt annoyed when he saw her.

"What! Is it you, Eponine?"

"Why do you speak to me so sternly? Have I done anything wrong to you?" she begged.

"No," he answered coldly.

"Well I, I thought that…"

"What? Tell me now-" Marius insisted.

Then she stopped. She attempted to smile and could not. She tried to resume:

"You said that…"

Then she was silent again and stood with her eyes cast down.

"Good night, Sir Marius," she said abruptly as she turned and walked away.

CHAPTER 5: A FATHER BESTED

The next day was the 3rd of June, 1832. Marius, at nightfall, was following the same path as the evening before, with the same thoughts of love in his heart when he saw Eponine approaching him. Two days in a row? This was too much. He turned quickly and went a different way to Plumet Street.

Eponine followed him. She saw him push aside the bar of the grating, and slip into the garden.

She approached the grating, felt the bars one after another until she felt one slide easily out of place. She stepped inside the garden, and then walked over to the wall and sat down with her back to the wall.

For over an hour she just sat and listened, thinking of how much she loved Marius, and how much he didn't care if she was even alive. She could hear their voices far off on the other side of the garden.

About ten o'clock in the evening, three people arrived in Plumet Street.

One said in a low and threatening voice:

"I followed her here last evening, she must be scouting the house for herself."

A few moments later, there were a total of six men walking down Plumet Street toward the house.

They arrived at the garden gate and one said: "This is the house."

"Is there a dog in the garden?" asked another.

"How do we get in?" asked a third

"The grating is old," added a fourth.

"So much the better," said the fifth. "It will be easier to cut."

The sixth, who had not yet opened his mouth, began to examine the grating as Eponine had done an hour before, grasping each bar successively and shaking it carefully. He found the loose bar and just as he went to pull it out of place a hand came out of the garden and pushed him in the chest and a roughened voice said to him without crying out:

"There is a dog in this garden."

He squinted and saw a girl standing before him.

He stepped back and stammered:

"What is this creature?" He asked.

"Your daughter" answered another.

It was indeed Eponine who was speaking to her father Thenardier.

The five other men quickly gathered in close.

"What are you doing here? What do you want with us? Are you crazy?" exclaimed Thenardier, as much as one can exclaim in a whisper.

Eponine began to laugh and stepped through the gap in the gate and sprang to his neck to hug him.

"I am here, my darling father, because I am here. Is there any law against sitting in a garden? It is you who shouldn't be here. What are you coming here for? This house has nothing. There is nothing to do here. Hug me instead my dear father! What a long time since I have seen you! You are out of prison then?"

Thenardier tried to free himself from Eponine's arms, and muttered:

"Very well. You have hugged me. Yes, I am out. Now, be off."

But Eponine did not loosen her arms one bit.

"My darling father, how did you do it? Tell me about it! And my mother! Where is my mother? Give me some news of mamma."

Thenardier answered:

"She is well, I don't know, leave me alone, I tell you to be off."

"But dear father I have done you service on this occasion. I have learned all about this home. You would risk being imprisoned for nothing. I swear to you that there is nothing to be done in this house. They are very poor people, and it is a shanty where there isn't a single cent to steal."

"Very well!" cried Thenardier. "When we have turned the house over we will tell you what there is inside" and he pushed her to pass by.

She placed her back against the gate, faced the six bandits who were all armed as she said in a low and firm voice:

"Well, I... I won't have it."

They stopped astounded.

"If you go into the garden," she continued. "If you touch this grating, I shall cry out. I will knock on doors, I shall wake everybody up, I shall have all six of you arrested, I shall call the police myself."

“She wouldn’t do it,” said Thenardier in a low voice.

“Beginning with you, father!” She added. “You are men. Now, I am a woman. I am not afraid of you, not a bit. I tell you that you shall not go into this house. Go anywhere else you like, but don't come here, I forbid it!

Thenardier made a movement towards her.

“Get Back!” she screamed loudly, causing the six men to quickly slink away into the street.

At the corner they stopped.

“Where are we going to sleep tonight?”

“Under Paris,” answered Thenardier.

“Have you the key of the grating with you?”

“Always,” Thenardier replied.

They disappeared into the sewer.

CHAPTER 6: A DAY SACRIFICED

Marius was still in the garden with Cosette. Her eyes were red, she'd been crying.

"What is the matter?" he asked.

"This morning my father told me to arrange all my little affairs and to be ready. He said we are leaving a week from now, and that we should go perhaps to England."

Marius shuddered from head to foot.

"But it is monstrous!" exclaimed Marius. He asked in a feeble voice: "When would you start?"

"He didn't say."

"And when should you return?"

"He didn't say."

Marius arose, and said coldly:

"Cosette, shall you go to England? Shall you go?"

"What would you have me do?" she asked, clasping her hands.

"Very well," said Marius. "Then I shall go elsewhere."

"No! I will tell you where we go! Come and join me where I am!"

"Go with you? Are you mad? That takes money and I have none! Go to England? I couldn't even afford the passport!"

He threw himself against a tree which was nearby, feeling neither the tree which was chafing his skin, nor the fever which was hammering his temples. He stood that way a long time until at last he turned around and asked:

"Do you love me?"

"I adore you. Do you love me, too?" she asked.

He caught her hand.

"Cosette, I have never given my word of honor to anybody. Now, I give you my most sacred word of honor. In memory of my father, I tell you that if you go away, I shall die."

Cosette trembled.

"Now listen," he said, "do not expect me tomorrow."

"Why not?"

"Do not expect me till the day after tomorrow!"

"Oh! why not?"

"You will see."

"A day without seeing you! Why, that is impossible."

"Let us sacrifice one day to gain perhaps a whole life."

Marius continued:

"In case something happens, you need to know my address. I live with a friend named Coferac on Verie Street, number 16."

He put his hand in his pocket, took out a knife, and wrote with the blade in the plastering of the wall:

"16, Verie Street."

Cosette, meanwhile, began to look into his eyes again.

"Expect me day after tomorrow" he said.

Then without saying a word they fell into each other's arms.

When Marius left the street was empty. Eponine had already chased away the bandits and left herself.

Marius now walked with certain step. He had thought of a new option while leaning against the tree. Though it seemed impossible, he had formed a desperate plan.

Chapter 7: Old Versus Young

Grandfather Gillenormand was now ninety-one and quite ill. He still lived with Mademoiselle Gillenormand in that old house which belonged to him. Four years now he had been waiting for Marius to come back. Today, Marius finally arrived.

Gillenormand told his servant in a feeble voice: "Show him in."

Gillenormand sat there, his head shaking, his eyes fixed on the door. It opened. Marius stepped into the doorway.

Grandfather Gillenormand thought him handsome, noble, striking, mature; a complete man. He would gladly have opened his arms, called to Marius, rushed upon him and begged his forgiveness, but all that came out of the old man's mouth was:

"Why have you come here?"

Marius answered with embarrassment:

"Sir-"

Gillenormand wanted Marius to stay. He wanted to love him and cry for him, but his stubborn old ways wouldn't let that through. He interrupted Marius with a sharp tone:

"I asked you why you are here. Do you come to ask my pardon? Have you seen your fault?"

Marius cast down his eyes and answered: "No, Sir."

"And so," exclaimed the old man impetuously,

"what do you want with me?"

"I come to ask your permission to marry."

"You! Marry? At twenty-one? You're poor! You can't afford it! Is the girl rich?"

"Same as me." Marius whispered.

"What! No dowry?"

"No."

"No money to her name? The two of you would be completely worthless!"

Marius plead: "I implore you! I beg of you, in the name of heaven, with clasped hands, Sir, I throw myself at your feet, allow me to marry her! Please Father!"

That single word, 'father,' said by Marius, caused his grandfather to pause. That word changed everything. Suddenly the old man's face changed to a smile and he walked over to Marius and said "Tell me about her. Come, tell me about your love scrapes, jabber-on, tell me all!

"Father," resumed Marius-

The old man's whole face shone with an unspeakable radiance.

"Yes! That is it! Call me father!"

Marius was astounded.

"Well, father, I love her. I have watched her for ages and now at last I see her every day. But now her father wants to take her to England. When I found out I said to myself: I will go and see my grandfather and tell him about her. If I cannot be with her I should die, I should make myself sick, I should throw myself into the river. I must marry her because if not I will go crazy."

Grandfather Gillenormand, radiant with joy, had sat down by Marius' side. He listened to Marius, enjoying the sound of his voice.

"So, her father doesn't know about it. That is all right. I have had adventures like that myself. More than one," admitted Gillenormand. "Do you know how we do it right? We don't rush in; we don't get married. We have good sense. We come and find our wealthy grandfather and play with his money until both the money and the girl are gone, then we move on. Here are two thousand dollars," Gillenormand said as he held out the money. "Amuse yourself! Don't marry the girl, play!"

Marius shook his head in horror.

He rose, picked up his hat which was on the floor, and walked towards the door with a firm and assured step. There he turned, bowed profoundly before his grandfather, raised his head again, and said:

"Five years ago, you insulted my father; to-day you have insulted my fiancée. I will ask nothing of you ever again Sir. Goodbye."

Grandfather Gillenormand was silent in shock. He stretched out his arms, attempted to rise, but before he could utter a word, the door closed and Marius had disappeared.

The old man cried out: "Help! help!"

His daughter appeared, then the servants. Gillenormand cried out with a pitiful rattle in his voice:

"Run after him! Catch him! What have I done to him! Oh! My God! My God! He is leaving and this time he will not come back!"

He went to the window, opened it with his trembling hands and stretched more than half his body outside as he cried out: "Marius Come Back! Marius! Marius! Marius!"

Chapter 8: Warnings

That very day, about four o'clock in the afternoon, Jean Valjean was sitting alone on the bank of the river. He wore his working-man's coat, brown linen trousers, and his cap with the long visor to hide his face. Valjean was worried.

Earlier that week he had seen Thenardier. Thanks to Valjean's disguise, Thenardier had not recognized him; but since then Jean Valjean had seen him again several times, and he was now certain that Thenardier was prowling about the neighborhood.

To make matters worse, Paris was not quiet. The political troubles had made the police become very active, and very secret. In trying to track down men in hiding, they would be very likely to discover a man like Jean Valjean.

He had decided to leave Paris, even the whole country of France. They would move to England. He had already told Cosette. In less than a week he wished to be gone. He was sitting on the banks of the river thinking of all these troubles: Thenardier, the police, the journey, Cosette, and the difficulty of procuring a passport. He was anxious about everything, but the most concerning thing he had found that morning. He had been walking in the garden before Cosette awoke when he noticed something scratched upon the garden wall, probably with a nail:

"16, Verie Street."

It was quite new, leaving white lines in the old black mortar. What was it? An address? A signal for others? A warning for him? Either way, someone had been in his garden, and was leaving messages. This was too much. He and Cosette must leave.

While he sat on the river bank thinking of all these new worries he noticed a shadow of a person standing behind him. He was about to turn around, when a folded paper fell between his knees, as if a hand had dropped it from above his head. He took the paper, unfolded it, and read:

Leave Paris, NOW!

Jean Valjean rose hastily and looked around, he barely saw someone, larger than a child, smaller than a man, dressed in a grey blouse and trousers, running away. He chased after the boy until suddenly the stranger jumped over a wall and slid down the bank toward the river. The note thrower was gone. Jean Valjean returned home immediately, full of fear.

Marius had left M. Gillenormand's house in despair.

He began to walk the streets, letting his mind meander aimlessly for hours. At two o'clock in the morning he had returned to Coferac's, and threw himself, fully clothed, upon his mattress.

When he half awoke in the morning, he saw his friends standing in the room, their hats upon their heads, all ready to go out, and very busy: Coferac, Enjolras, Comfehr and others.

Coferac said to him:

"Are you going to the funeral of General Lamark?"

Marius was so tired and depressed that he didn't understand a word.

Marius didn't fully wake up until long after his friends were gone. He put into his pocket the loaded pistols which Javert had given him months before and walked out of the house. He had a furnace burning in his brain and could think of nothing other than Cosette. At nine that night he walked toward her house, knowing he was going to see her for the last time.

When he arrived at her house he removed the loose bar and walked into the garden. Cosette was not at the place where she usually waited for him. He crossed the garden and went to the seat near the steps. Cosette was not there. He raised his eyes, and saw the shutters of the house were closed. He suddenly looked around the garden and noticed that the house was deserted. He ran up to the door and knocked. When no one answered he rapped again louder, then he ran to the window and pounded on the shutters so hard they nearly shattered. He raised his voice and cried out "Cosette!" He cried her name long and loud as he began to sob in agony. There was no answer. She was gone.

Marius now felt completely empty. His grandfather had abandoned him and now his only love had done the same. Marius wished he could just lay down and die.

Suddenly he heard a voice calling out from the street:

"Sir Marius!"

He sat up.

"Who's there?" he said.

"Sir Marius, is it you?"

"Yes." he said getting up and looking around the garden.

"Sir Marius," added the voice, "your friends are expecting you at the barricade, in Chanvrie Road. Hurry, you are late."

This voice seemed familiar to him. Marius ran to the grating, pushed aside the movable bar, passed his head through, and saw somebody who appeared to him to be a young man dressed in grey blouse and trousers, rapidly disappearing in the distance.

CHAPTER 9: TO THE BARRICADES

In the spring of 1832 Paris was like a bomb just waiting for a spark to ignite the fuse. In June, that spark was the death of General Lamark.

Many of the citizens of Paris had loved the Emperor Napoleon and hated life under the King. They had been waiting for the right time to overthrow the King and make Napoleon their leader once again.

General Lamark had been a great soldier. He had always been a friend of the people, and they had made him into their own national hero. When he died, they had decided his funeral would start a revolution. The friends of the ABC weren't the only ones to rise up in revolt. At Lamark's funeral they were joined by students from the law School the medical school and many colleges. They were joined by refugees from many nations: Spain, Italy, Germany and Poland. Together they all stood, staring at the National Guard soldiers who were escorting the coffin.

As tension mounted suddenly a gun shot rang out. One of the National Guardsmen fell to the ground dead.

Once shots were fired there was no turning back. A battle began with people firing and fighting on all sides. Thousands of young men ran into empty streets and dead-end roads to set up barricades. In less than an hour twenty-seven barricades rose from the ground. Coferac, Enjolras, Comfehr, Jean Prouvaire and others fled to Chanvrie Road to set up their own barricade. They picked up supporters along the way, including one very helpful gentleman fighting for them in Billettes street. They brought him along to Chanvrie Road and together they all built a massive barricade. The front of the barricade was made of everything they could find. There were doors, piles of paving-stones, barrels tied together with boards stuck through the wheels of a cart and an overturned bus. Anything that could block a bullet was thrown on the pile and the barricade grew higher and higher.

Enjolras directed the building of the main barricade in front as well as the smaller barricades to close the little side streets. Enjolras only left one road open, a back alley called Mondetour street. This was to make sure they could escape if needed.

The final touch on the massive barricade was to place a huge red flag on top of a long pole sticking out of the top of the barricade. It waved proudly in the wind, proclaiming their freedom from the King.

The young men got down to business, handing out the rest of the guns as well as all the bullets. They didn't have much; only 30 bullets for each man. They knew the King had more bullets, more men, and more guns. Who would the King send to fight them? The police? The National Guard? The Army? The insurgents didn't care. They were fighting for freedom. With stern faces and iron resolve they waited.

Enjolras was restless. He went to find Gavroche who was counting bullets in the basement of the wine shop.

The man from Billettes street had just entered the basement room and Gavroche followed him with his eyes. When the man had sat down, the boy arose quickly and walked right past the man to look at him closer.

Gavroche said to himself: *"Can it be? No, it isn't! Why yes!"*

Suddenly Gavroche felt himself grasped by large arms and turned about.

"You are small," said Enjolras, "nobody will see you. Go out of the barricades, glide along by the houses, look about the streets a little, and come and tell me what is going on."

Gavroche straightened himself up.

"Little folks are good for something then!" Gavroche said proudly. "I will go! In the meantime, trust the little folks, distrust the big ones."

Gavroche, raising his head and lowering his voice, added, pointing to the man from Billettes street:

"You see that big fellow there?"

"Yes, so?"

"He is a spy."

"Are you sure?" asked Enjolras.

"It was only two weeks ago he was arresting me for stealing some wallets over on Royal Bridge."

Enjolras hastily left the boy and whispered a few

words to a comrade. The two men went out of the room and returned almost immediately, accompanied by three others. The five men walked with guns in hand toward the volunteer from Billettes street.

"Who are you?" asked Enjolras abruptly.

The man looked straight into Enjolras' eye and knew that he was found out. He smiled.

"I am an officer of the government."

"Your name is?"

"Inspector Javert."

Before Javert had time to turn around, he was collared, thrown down, bound, and searched.

They took his badge, watch and wallet. Then they tied him to a post in the middle of the basement-room.

Gavroche, who had witnessed the whole scene and approved with silent nods of his head, approached Javert and said to him:

"Looks like this time the mouse has caught the cat."

Gavroche then ran out to do his duty as Enjolras had ordered.

CHAPTER 10: BLOOD FOR BLOOD

No battle yet. The clock of Saint Merry had struck ten. In the midst of this quiet, tense night, a young cheerful voice began to sing the old popular song, Clair de Lune.

Enjolras turned to Comfehr:

"It is Gavroche," said Enjolras.

"He is warning us," said Comfehr.

Gavroche bounded into the barricade breathless, saying:

"Where's my gun, they're right behind me!"

Every man took his post for the combat.

Forty-three insurgents, among them Enjolras, Comfehr, Coferac, Jean Prouvaire, and Gavroche were on their knees in the great barricade, their heads peeking over or through the barricade, ready to fire.

They heard the sound of steps, measured, heavy, numerous. The sound grew louder and louder but they still couldn't see the soldiers marching toward them.

They heard a voice cry out:

"Who is there?"

Enjolras answered in a lofty and ringing tone:

"French Revolution!"

"Fire!" said the voice.

A flash erupted into the street as if the door of a furnace were opened and suddenly closed.

A fearful explosion burst over the barricade. The

red flag fell as the post was shattered by bullets.

Everything was then oddly silent. There was no more shooting and no more footsteps. Enjolras and Comfehr tended to the wounded until they heard Gavroche yell: "Take care!"

Municipal Guards had snuck in over the barricade and were right on top of them. The moment was critical. Coferac was on his back with a gun in his face crying "Help!" The largest municipal guard of all marched toward Gavroche. The Guard raised his bayonet to slice the child to bits when suddenly the bayonet fell from his hands. A bullet had struck the Municipal Guard in the middle of the forehead and he fell on his back. A second ball struck the other Guard just before he could kill Coferac. The bullet hit him right in the chest and he fell dead to the pavement. Who had shot these men?

It was Marius. He had finally entered the barricade. By the first shot he had saved Gavroche, and by the second delivered Coferac.

On the summit of the barricade could now be seen thronging Municipal Guards, soldiers of the Line, National Guards, all with guns in hand. They already covered more than two-thirds of the wall, but they did not leap down in; they seemed to hesitate, fearing some trap. Marius threw down his now empty pistols as he noticed a keg of powder behind him next to the wine shop. As he turned to run for it, a soldier aimed at him. A hand appeared on the muzzle of the soldier's gun and stopped the bullet. It was the hand of the young working-man wearing the grey blouse and trousers. The shot went off, passed through the hand, and perhaps also through the working-man, for he fell, but the bullet did not reach Marius.

All the other municipal guards raised their guns as an officer extended his sword and said:

"Take aim!"

Suddenly, a thundering voice was heard much louder than the officers:

"Be gone, or I'll blow up the barricade!"

Everyone turned towards the voice.

Marius had climbed the barricade and set the keg of powder in the center. Now the National Guards, Municipal Guards, officers, and soldiers watched with horror, as Marius lowered a torch toward the powder, while uttering another cry:

"Be gone, or I'll blow up the barricade!"

"Blow up the barricade?" said a sergeant, "and yourself also!"

Marius answered:

"Yes, and myself also."

Marius lowered a torch down right next to the keg of powder, and soon there were no more guards on the barricade as they ran as fast as possible to the far end of the street.

The barricade was saved.

All the insurgents flocked round Marius.

Coferac hugged him tightly: "You're here!"

"Just in time!" said Comfehr.

"Without you I should have been dead!"

continued Coferac.

"Without you I'd been gobbled!" added Gavroche.

They kept slapping Marius on the back until they realized that one of them was missing.

One of the most valiant young men, Jean Prouvaire, was nowhere to be found. They searched among the wounded, in the wine shop, and among the dead, he was not there. He was evidently a prisoner.

Comfehr said to Enjolras:

"They have our friend; we have their officer. We must trade. I am going to tie my handkerchief to my cane, and go with a flag of truce to offer their man for ours."

"Listen," said Enjolras, laying his hand on Comfehr's arm.

There was a significant clicking of arms at the end of the street.

They heard a man's voice cry:

"Long Live France!"

They recognized it, it was Prouvaire's voice.

There was a flash and an explosion.

Silence reigned again.

"They have killed him," exclaimed Comfehr.

Enjolras looked at Javert and said to him:

"With that shot, the army just sealed your fate; blood for blood."

Chapter 11: A Wounded Hand

While all the others were gathering around Javert, Marius thought of the little barricade at the escape route, and went to check it. It was completely unguarded, so he stood as sentry there to keep his friends safe.

He heard his name called out faintly: "Sir Marius!"

He recognized the voice. It was the same voice that had been at Cosette's house telling him to go to the barricade. He looked about him and saw nobody.

"Sir Marius!" repeated the voice, "at your feet."

He looked down to see someone lying on the pavement wearing a pair of torn trousers, bare feet, and a blouse that looked covered in blood. Marius caught a glimpse of a pale face and asked:

"Eponine?"

Marius bent down quickly. He hadn't recognized her before because she was dressed like a man. "What are you doing there?"

"I am dying," she said.

Marius exclaimed: "You are wounded! Wait, I will carry you into the wine shop! They will dress your wounds! Is it serious?"

He tried to take her hand to lift her but she cried out in pain.

He looked at her hand and saw in the center a black hole.

"What happened to your hand?" he asked.

"A bullet."

"How?"

"Did you see a gun aimed at you?"

"Yes, and a hand stopped it."

"The hand was mine," she whispered.

Marius shuddered. "Poor child! But that is not so bad, you'll get better. People don't die from a shot in the hand."

She murmured:

"The bullet passed through my hand, but it went out through my back. I'm dying. Will you sit with me?"

He sat down immediately and she laid her head on Marius' knees, and without looking at him, she said:

"Oh! how good you are. How kind! I don't suffer any more!"

She remained a moment in silence, then she turned her head with effort and looked at Marius.

"Do you know, Sir Marius? I was worried when I showed you that garden that you would love her. I had hoped that maybe you would still have some love left for me. When I saw the man aiming at you, I put up my hand upon the muzzle of the gun because I wanted to die before you. Now I am well. Do you remember the day when I came into your room? Do you remember, Sir Marius?"

Her torn blouse showed her bare throat. While she was talking Marius could see her bleeding more and more; he knew she didn't have long.

Marius looked on her with profound compassion.

"Oh!" she exclaimed suddenly, "it is coming back. I am dying!" She seized her blouse and bit it, and her legs writhed upon the pavement.

At this moment the voice of little Gavroche resounded through the barricade. The child had mounted upon a table to load his musket and was gaily singing a popular song.

Eponine raised herself up, and listened, then she murmured:

"That's my brother, isn't it?"

"Your brother?" asked Marius. "The one who is singing?"

"Yes, he is singing my requiem. It will not be long now!"

She added with a strange expression: "Listen, I don't want to deceive you. I have a letter in my pocket for you. I was told to put it in the mail but I kept it. I didn't want it to reach you."

She handed him a letter from her pocket and added: Now promise me-"

"What?" asked Marius.

"Promise to kiss me on the forehead when I am dead. I shall feel it."

"I promise you."

She let her head fall back upon Marius' knees and her eyelids closed. He thought that poor soul had gone when she whispered out: "Do you know, Sir Marius, I believe I was a little in love with you."

She smiled again and expired.

Marius kept his promise. He kissed her cold forehead, and lowered her gently to the ground. Then he ran to the wine shop so he could have light to read the letter:

"To Sir Marius Pontmercy, at M. Coferac's, Verie Street, No. 16.

My beloved, Alas! My father wishes to start immediately. We shall be tonight in Homme Street, No. 7. In a week we shall be in England.

COSETTE. June 4th."

What had happened?

Eponine had done all she could to keep Marius from Cosette. After making her father Thenardier and his crew flee Cosette's house, Eponine changed into boy's clothing and threw a note to Valjean saying:

Leave Paris, NOW.

Later that night Cosette had written a letter to Marius but had no way to get it to him. She saw this "boy" outside her gate and gave the letter to him with $5 to deliver it to Marius' address. Eponine had put the letter in her pocket, never intending to give it to Marius. When the revolution had started she had decided that if she could not have him, nobody would!

She went to find him at Cosette's empty house

and gave him instructions to go to the barricade, knowing he would die there. She had, for that moment, wanted him dead. Only when she saw the gun aimed at his face did she change her mind, and take the bullet herself. Now he was still at the barricade, still likely to die, but her last act had been one of love.

CHAPTER 12: LETTERS

Marius covered Cosette's letter with kisses, but nothing had really changed.

Her father was still taking her to England, his grandfather still refused to consent to the marriage, and Marius was still at the barricade, likely to die. He thought that there were still two duties for him to fulfill before he died: to inform Cosette of his death, and to save this poor child, Eponine's brother and Thenardier's son, from the imminent catastrophe. He hadn't honored his father by saving Thenardier, nor the daughter Eponine, but Marius could still save Thenardier's son, Gavroche.

Marius took out some paper and wrote these few lines:

"Our marriage was impossible. I have asked my grandfather, he has refused; I am without fortune, and you also. I ran to your house, I did not find you, and without you I die. I love you. When you read this, my soul will be near you, and will smile upon you."

Having nothing to seal this letter with, he merely folded the paper, and wrote upon it this address:

"To Mademoiselle Cosette Fosh, Homme Street, No. 7."

Then he took one more piece of paper and wrote on it:

My name is Marius Pontmercy.

Carry my corpse to my grandfather's house.
M. Gillenormand, Calvary Street, No. 6.

He put that note into his coat-pocket, then he called for Gavroche. The boy ran up with his joyous and devoted face:

"Yes, Sir Marius?"

"Will you do something for me?"

"Anything," said Gavroche. "Without you, I should have been cooked, sure."

"You see this letter?"

"Yes."

"Take it. Leave the barricade immediately, and tomorrow morning you will carry it to the address written here, to Mademoiselle Cosette Fosh, Homme Street No. 7."

The heroic boy answered: "But if I do that I'll miss all the fighting! How about I leave in the morning?"

"It will be too late. The barricade will probably be completely surrounded and you won't get out. Go, right away!"

Gavroche had nothing more to say; he stood there scratching his ear till suddenly he took the letter and said "All right."

As he ran down a side street he already had a plan in mind. "It is hardly midnight" he thought. "Homme Street is not far away. I will take the letter there right away and I shall get back in time for the fighting."

Jean Valjean, at that very moment was sitting on his porch in Homme Street, worrying. They had fled to this house in a hurry, bringing almost nothing with them. Cosette was terribly depressed, and had argued with him and fought the whole way.

He had brought nothing but the little box Cosette called "the inseparable." Toussaint, the maid, had packed up a few clothes including Valjean's National Guard uniform and Cosette herself had brought only her writing-desk.

It was there that Valjean had just seen these lines written:

My beloved, alas! My father wishes to start immediately. We shall be tonight in the Homme Street No. 7. In a week we shall be in London.

COSETTE. June 4th.

When Valjean saw the imprint of those words on her writing desk he was aghast. Cosette had told someone their address. Valjean knew instantly who it was. He didn't know the boy's name, but he knew who he was. The unknown prowler from the Luxembourg, that wretched seeker of romance, that imbecile who had followed them home.

Jean Valjean now felt something new: Hatred

He sat on the steps of his new house, thinking of this young man; thinking of how Cosette had deceived him, and how much happier they would be once they arrived in England.

Valjean looked toward the center of Paris where

he could hear explosions and gun fire. Then he saw somebody coming up the street. A little boy was skipping up the street, throwing rocks at the lamps to break them, and then squinting to see house numbers.

"Little boy," said Valjean, "what are you doing?"

Gavroche looked at Valjean and replied: "Little yourself."

"Poor creature," thought Jean Valjean, *"he is probably just hungry."*

Valjean offered the boy a five-dollar bill and told him to go buy some food.

As Gavroche put the five dollars in his pocket he asked: "Do you live on this street?"

"Yes; why."

"Could you show me number seven?"

"What do you want with number seven?"

Here the boy stopped; he feared that he had said too much. He stammered out "Ah...um..."

An idea flashed across Jean Valjean's mind. He said to the child:

"Have you brought the letter I am waiting for?"

"You?" said Gavroche. "You are not a woman."

"The letter is for Mademoiselle Cosette; isn't it?"

"Cosette?" muttered Gavroche, "yes, I believe it is that funny name."

"Well," resumed Valjean, "I am here to deliver the letter to her. Give it to me."

Gavroche drew out a folded paper and handed it to Valjean.

"That letter comes from the barricade in Chanvrie

Road," Gavroche said. "I am going back there now. Good night, citizen."

This said, Gavroche plunged back into the darkness as if he made a hole in it, disappearing instantly from sight.

Jean Valjean went in with Marius' letter, climbed the stairs, and lit a candle. He read the letter, reading the last line over and over again"

"-I die. I love you. When you read this, my soul will be near you, and will smile upon you."

Valjean uttered a hideous cry of inward joy. So, it was finished. The end came sooner than he had dared to hope. The being who threatened his destiny was disappearing. Marius was going away of himself, freely, of his own accord. Without any intervention on Jean Valjean's part, without any fault of his, "that man" was about to die, perhaps he was already dead.

At this moment a headache began in Valjean's brain.

"No. He is not dead yet."

The letter was evidently written to be read by Cosette in the morning; there hadn't been any recent gunfire, so it was likely the boy was still alive.

"Well, I just have to let things take their course. That man cannot escape. If he is not dead yet, it is certain that he will die. Good riddance to him and more happiness to us!"

Even as he said this he was already becoming more gloomy.

He knew he was telling himself lies. He couldn't just let the boy die. He couldn't betray Cosette's love like that.

Ten minutes later Valjean left his house in the full dress of a National Guardsman. He had a loaded gun and a box full of ammunition. He jogged quickly towards the sound of the fighting.

PART FIVE: JEAN VALJEAN

Chapter 1: Five Less and One More

Enjolras had assessed their chances and knew it was hopeless. Everyone in the barricade was going to die. There was no escape now.

"The whole army of Paris fights against us." He told them. "There is the National Guard along with the Fifth and Sixth Legion. We will be attacked within the hour. As for the people of Paris; they were with us yesterday but this morning they do not stir. No one is coming, we are abandoned."

All were struck dumb. There was a moment of inexpressible silence.

"Long live death! Let us all stay!" someone yelled.

"Why all?" said Enjolras. "Some of you are fathers, the only provider for your household. We will be remembered whether there are 40 dead or 30 dead here tomorrow.

Enjolras held out in his hands four National Guard uniforms which he had saved. "If you wear these uniforms, they'll let you out, thinking you are among their ranks." How many of you are the only support for your families?"

After some arguing about honor and duty, five men stepped forward, but there were only four uniforms.

"One must stay," said Enjolras as the five men all started arguing that they should have the honor of dying, of staying with their friends.

At this moment a fifth uniform dropped, as if from heaven, upon the four others.

Marius raised his eyes and saw Cosette's father. He had entered the barricade unnoticed wearing his National Guard Uniform, heard the argument, and taken it off to give to another man.

Now all five fathers would be saved.

"Who is this man?" asked Enjolras.

Marius said in a grave voice:

"I know him."

Marius' word was enough assurance for all.

Enjolras turned towards Jean Valjean:

"Citizen, you are welcome, but you know that we are going to die."

Jean Valjean, without answering, helped the father whom he saved to put on the uniform.

Marius now had even more questions than ever. How did Cosette's father end up here? What did he come to do? Mr. Fosh did not speak to him, did not look at him, and had not even the appearance of hearing him when Marius said: "I know him."

Once the five fathers had gone, Jean Valjean went into the wine shop to get a drink. Comfehr said to him "it's lucky for you Marius recognized you, the last volunteer we had was a spy. That's him tied to that post."

Valjean looked over and in shock, recognized Javert. Javert did not even flinch in surprise. He haughtily dropped his eyelids, and merely said: "Nature makes things so simple"

A cry came from the barricade: "Cannon!" All men rushed out just in time to see a cannon stop at the end of the street aimed at the center of the barricade. All the insurgents ducked their heads as they saw the fuse lit. Just as they expected a cannonball to come roaring through, they saw instead, Gavroche come tumbling into the barricade from one of the side streets. The cannon erupted, but Gavroche produced more effect in the barricade than the cannonball.

The cannonball stuck in the barricade and never broke through. Seeing this, the entire mass of insurgents began to laugh.

The men surrounded Gavroche, cheering him as if he had singlehandedly stopped the cannonball.

Marius, shuddering, took him aside.

"Who told you to come back? Did you carry my letter to its address?"

"Citizen, your lady was asleep. I delivered it to the house, she will get the letter when she wakes up."

Marius was happy for Cosette but sad for Gavroche. He watched the boy bound away to warn his "comrades" as he called them, that the barricade was surrounded. Gavroche had had great difficulty in getting in and told them all that no one could now get out.

CHAPTER 2: GRAPESHOT

Enjolras watched as the cannon was reloaded, but this time it was not a cannonball, but rather canisters of grapeshot. Grapeshot is a canvas bag filled with small metal balls or slugs, meant to spread out in every direction and cause widespread damage instead of one big shot.

Enjolras watched as the cannon turned its aim slightly to the side and saw the match drop down toward the fuse.

"Heads down, keep close to the wall!" cried Enjolras. "Everyone on your knees along the barricade!"

The insurgents, who were scattered in front of the wine-shop, and who had left their posts on Gavroche's arrival, rushed pell-mell towards the barricade; but they didn't make it before the cannon fired the grapeshot.

The shot hit the side wall right where there was a small gap between the wall and the barricade. The grapeshot balls ricocheted off the wall and flew behind the barricade killing two men and wounding three more.

Enjolras knew that the barricade would be overtaken in no time. It was strong against men, cannonballs, and bullets, but not grapeshot.

Enjolras told Comfehr they needed something to put in the gap to block the grapeshot, something that wouldn't let the balls ricochet. Valjean overheard the conversation and remembered seeing that an old woman hang a mattress on the outside of her window, trying to keep her windows from being broken by the battle below.

This window was just a little outside of the barricade. The mattress had been hung from two ropes which, in the distance, seemed like small threads.

"Can somebody lend me a double-barreled rifle?" asked Jean Valjean.

Enjolras, who had just reloaded his, handed it over. Jean Valjean aimed at the window and fired.

One of the two ropes of the mattress was cut.

The mattress now hung only by one thread.

Jean Valjean fired the second barrel. The second rope snapped in half as the mattress slid down the wall and fell into the street. Jean Valjean quickly went out at the opening, entered the street and ran through a storm of bullets fired by the army at the other end of the street. Valjean went to the mattress, picked it up, put it on his back, and returned to the barricade.

He put the mattress into the opening himself. He fixed it against the wall, dove behind the barricade, and ducked, awaiting the next grapeshot.

He didn't have to wait long.

The cannon vomited its grapeshot with a roar. But there was no ricochet. The grape shot stuck in the mattress.

The barricade was once again, saved.

"Citizen," said Enjolras to Jean Valjean, "the republic thanks you."

Comfehr admired and laughed. He exclaimed:

"Glory to the mattress which nullifies a cannon!"

All the men cheered except Coferac who had just noticed Gavroche climbing out over the barricade. "What are you doing?" whispered Coferac loudly.

Gavroche cocked up his nose.

"Citizen, I am filling my basket." He was collecting unused bullets left behind by the dead soldiers on the other side of the barricade. He knew the insurgents were almost out, and he was determined to do his part.

Coferac cried: "Come back! The grapeshot!"

"Shortly," said Gavroche with a bound as he sprang into the street.

Twenty dead soldiers lay in the street, each with at least 20 bullets in their pockets. Gavroche went from soldier to soldier taking their bullets. The smoke in the street was like a fog which hid Gavroche from being noticed. That is, until he started singing.

Joy is my character,
'Tis the fault of Voltaire;
Misery is my trousseau,
'Tis the fault of Rousseau.

A bullet zinged passed his head. Gavroche looked up and sang even louder. Then a second shot whirred past him. The third hit his basket full of bullets, spilling it out. He bent down, picked it up, and refilled it singing even louder:

Gavroche responded to each bullet by singing a new verse to his song. The National Guards and the soldiers laughed as they aimed at him. He lay down, then rose up, hid himself in a doorway, then sprang out, disappeared, reappeared, escaped, returned, repulsed the army by making silly faces at them, and meanwhile kept taking bullets off dead soldiers. The insurgents, breathless with anxiety, followed him with their eyes. The barricade was trembling, yet Gavroche was still singing. The bullets ran after him but he was more nimble than they. He was playing an indescribably terrible game of hide-and-seek with death.

One bullet, however, better aimed or more treacherous than the others, reached the care-free child. Gavroche tottered and fell. The whole barricade gave a cry; but Gavroche had fallen only to rise again. He sat up, raised both arms in the air, looked in the direction whence the shot came, and began to sing:

I have fallen to the earth,
'Tis the fault of Voltaire;
With my nose in the gutter,
'Tis the fault of . . .

He did not finish. A second bullet from the same marksman cut him short. This time he fell with his face upon the pavement, and did not stir again. That little great soul had at last taken flight.

Marius sprang out of the barricade. Comfehr followed him, but it was too late. Gavroche was dead. Comfehr brought back the basket of bullets; Marius brought back the child.

WHY! thought Marius. *Thenardier brought back my father living, while I have brought back his child dead.*

When Marius re-entered the wine-shop with Gavroche in his arms, his face, like the child's, was covered with blood.

Just as he had stooped down to pick up Gavroche, a bullet had grazed his skull; he hadn't even noticed it.

CHAPTER 3: VALJEAN TAKES REVENGE

When the bullets from Gavroche's basket were distributed, every man had fifteen more. Enjolras put one of the bullets in a pistol and laid it on the table near Javert.

Enjolras was furious now. "The last man to leave this room will kill the spy!"

Jean Valjean suddenly appeared in the wine shop and said to Enjolras:

"You are the commander?"

"Yes."

"You thanked me for getting the mattress and saving the barricade from grapeshot."

"The barricade has two saviors, Marius Pontmercy and you."

"Do you think that I deserve a reward?"

"Certainly."

"Well, I ask one."

"What?"

"To kill that man myself."

Javert raised his head, saw Jean Valjean and said:

"That is just."

As for Enjolras, he had begun to reload his rifle as he said:

"No objection. Take the spy."

Jean Valjean picked up the pistol, and a slight click announced that he had cocked it.

Javert walked bound ahead of Valjean out of the wine shop where they passed Marius as they walked around the corner to a little alley where they could not be seen.

Once they reached the little side barricade Valjean turned Javert around so they were facing each other.

"Take your revenge," said Javert through gritted teeth.

Jean Valjean put the pistol under his arm and took a knife out of his pocket.

"A blade!" exclaimed Javert. "You are right. That suits you better."

Jean Valjean cut the ropes which Javert had about his neck, then he cut the ropes which bound his wrists, and said to him:

"You are free."

Javert stood astonished and confused.

Jean Valjean continued:

"I don't expect to leave this place alive. Still, if by chance I survive, I live under the name of Fosh in the Homme Street, Number Seven."

Javert repeated in an undertone: "Number seven." He buttoned his coat, turned half 'round, folded his arms and walked off in the direction of the markets. Jean Valjean followed him with his eyes. After a few steps, Javert turned back, and cried to Jean Valjean:

"Kill me instead, do not torture me like this."

"Go away," said Jean Valjean.

Javert walked backwards with slow steps. A moment afterwards, he turned the corner.

When Javert was gone, Jean Valjean fired the pistol in the air.

Then he re-entered the barricade and said: "It is done."

When Marius saw Jean Valjean return alone he asked Enjolras:

"The police officer. Do you know his name?"

"Of course. He told us. It was Inspector Javert."

A dreary chill passed through the heart of Marius. He remembered Javert. The inspector had given him the pistols he had just used to save two of his friends.

CHAPTER 4: TAKEN PRISONER

The drum beat the charge. The time had come.

The attack on the barricade came like a hurricane. A mass of hundreds of soldiers followed by hundreds more came running toward the barricade. Drums beating, trumpets sounding, bayonets fixed; they came straight upon the barricade like a battering ram.

The barricade was a mass of flashes; guns firing on all sides faster than anyone could take aim.

The army had more men, the insurgents had more spirit. There was assault after assault. As one row of soldiers was cut down by bullets, another row appeared right behind them to continue the fight.

They fought with pistols, swords, knives and fists. The front of the wine house was riddled with bullets. Coferac was killed; Comfehr was stabbed in the chest by three men at once. Dozens more died in minutes.

Marius, still fighting, was so hacked with wounds, that his face could not be recognized through all the blood. Enjolras alone was untouched. When his weapon failed, he reached his hand to right or left, and a fellow insurgent put whatever weapon he could in his grasp.

The barricade was finally broken apart by the cannon, now firing at close range. As they knew they'd be killed instantly without a barricade, the rest of the insurgents ran into the wine shop for protection. Enjolras now used his empty rifle as a cane to beat down the soldiers' bayonets as he closed the door behind him.

Marius was the only one left outside. A bullet had broken his shoulder-blade and he felt that he was fainting, falling to the ground for the last time. At that moment, his eyes already closed, he felt a vigorous hand seizing him. As he lost consciousness his last thought was of Cosette as he seemed to say to her: "I am taken prisoner. I shall be shot."

In the wine shop, Enjolras barricaded the door, but it was broken down in minutes.

His men were cut down one by one until at last he was the only one left. Without ammunition, without a sword, he had now in his hand only the barrel of his rifle.

"Shoot me." said Enjolras as he threw away the rifle stump so he could pull his shirt open, presenting his bare chest to the soldiers.

Twelve soldiers lined up and aimed their rifles.

The sergeant cried: "Take aim!"

"Long Live the Republic!" shouted Enjolras.

Enjolras' face broke into a smile as the last of the shots rang out.

Pierced by twelve bullets he bowed his head in death.

CHAPTER 5: DARKNESS

Marius truly was taken prisoner. The prisoner of Jean Valjean.

Valjean had taken no part in the combat other than to save others. Whenever a man fell, Valjean carried him into the wine shop and bandaged his wounds. During the attacks he had never taken his eyes off Marius. When a shot struck down Marius, Jean Valjean ran to him with the speed of a tiger, picked him up, and carried him around the back of the wine shop. Valjean pried an iron grating from the ground and shimmied down into the sewer, pulling Marius in behind him.

I, the sewer itt was complete blackness, absolute silence, night.

Valjean looked at Marius but couldn't tell if he was alive or dead.

He heard soldiers above and realized they would soon find the open grate and follow him. Valjean lifted Marius onto his shoulder, turned and resolutely marched into the darkness.

To find his way was difficult. Groping and grasping in the dark he climbed his way through the refuse.

He had been walking for about half an hour when his arm holding Marius began to cramp. He hefted Marius onto the other shoulder, and plunged deeper into the darkness.

After hours of walking in the filthy muck, switching arms multiple times, Jean Valjean found he was exhausted, hungry and thirsty with no hope of relief.

He had no idea where he was going. Nothing told him what zone of the city he was passing through, nor what route he had followed. At times he heard the rumblings of the wagons above his head, but now there were no more wagons as he reached the outskirts of Paris. The further he walked from the center of Paris the worse the sewers became. The pavement was slipping away under him as years of rain had broken the pavement apart and it had disappeared in the mire of sewage.

He entered into this unstable slime. It was water on the surface, mud and muck at the bottom. The mire appeared not very deep for a few steps. But the further he advanced the more his feet sank in. He was knee deep in mud with water even higher. He walked on, holding Marius with both arms in front of him at chest level. Soon the mud rose above his knees, and the water was up to his waist. He knew he couldn't turn back now, he was too exhausted to make it back out of the mire. Valjean sank in deeper and deeper with every step. The water came up to his armpits and he felt that he was about to drown. He now held Marius over his head, and, with amazing strength he advanced. Soon he had only his head out of the water, his arms supporting Marius above his head

He sank still deeper, forcing Valjean to throw his

face back to escape the water and be able to breathe. This was the end. Valjean's face was about to slip beneath the water. He made a desperate last effort and thrust his foot forward into the abyss. His foot struck something solid; pavement!

Valjean ascended this broken pavement with superhuman strength till he reached the flat pavement and could see light. Valjean looked up and saw an outlet.

Feeling the victory of escape, the resurrection to life, Valjean pressed on to the outlet. He felt exhaustion no more, he felt Marius' weight no longer; he ran rather than walked to the outlet. Then he stopped.

It was indeed an outlet, but not for Valjean.

The exit was closed by a strong iron grating which was bolted shut with a sturdy lock.

Beyond the grating Valjean could see the open air, the river, the daylight, the beach. Valjean could almost taste freedom. He laid Marius along the wall and then clenched the bars with both hands; shaking them with all his might. The grating did not budge. The grate was invincible. What could he do? He could never make it back the way they had come. He had no strength. He could never make it through that mire again.

Valjean realized he had escaped the barricade only to enter a prison. It was over. All that Jean Valjean had done was useless.

He dropped to the ground face first beside the

motionless Marius. No exit. This was the last drop of anguish he could bare.

Who did he think about in this moment of despair? Not himself, not of Marius. He thought of Cosette.

Chapter 6: From Jailer to Jailer

Valjean felt a hand on his shoulder and heard a quiet voice which said:

"Go halves."

Somebody else was in the darkness, in this sewer? Jean Valjean thought he must be dreaming. Either that or he was already dead. He hadn't heard any footsteps. Was it possible? He raised his eyes and saw the horrible figure of Thenardier.

Thenardier bent down and tried to see Valjean's face, but due to the mud and the darkness, he couldn't recognize him.

"How are you going to manage to get out?" asked Thenardier, "Impossible to pick the lock. So, we go halves."

"What do you mean?" asked Valjean.

"Obviously you have killed this man; and I have the key to the grate."

Valjean began to understand. Thenardier thought he was an assassin.

Thenardier resumed:

"Listen, comrade. You haven't killed that man without looking through his pockets. Give me half of his money and I will open the door for you."

Jean Valjean felt in his pockets and found only a few coins. He turned out his pocket, all soaked with filth, and showed Thenardier the meager prize.

"You picked the wrong man to kill," said

Thenardier.

Thenardier bent down and felt Marius' coat pockets to be sure there was no more money, and without attracting Jean Valjean's attention, managed to tear off a strip of Marius' coat at the same time.

He took the money from Valjean's hand and then took the key from under his blouse.

"Now, friend, you are free to go."

The bolt slid and the door turned. Thenardier opened the door just enough for Jean Valjean to get through, then closed the grating again and locked the bolt with no noise made at all. As he looked through the grating at Valjean out in the light, he suddenly recognized him. "Just as well," Thenardier said to himself as he walked away down the sewer.

Jean Valjean was irresistibly overcome by the sense of freedom. He could see the sky, breath the air, and he could hear again. Jean Valjean couldn't help but gaze at that vast clear sky which was above him. He took in the majesty of the eternal heavens, and stood and offered a silent prayer. Then he scooped up a little water from the river and put it to Marius' lips. Marius' eyelids did not open; but his half-open mouth breathed and his lips moved.
He was still alive.

Jean Valjean now plunged his hand into the river again to drink, to wash, to return to the land of the living. Suddenly he felt an indescribable uneasiness; the kind felt when we have somebody behind us, that we didn't know was there.

Valjean turned around. A man of tall stature, wrapped in a long overcoat, with folded arms, and holding in his right hand a club stood erect a few steps behind Jean Valjean.

It was Javert.

CHAPTER 7: RETURN OF THE PRODIGAL SON

After his departure from the barricade, Javert had gone to the police station where he was tasked with following a bandit and fugitive well known to him, Thenardier. Javert had followed him all the way to the sewer where he had disappeared.

Thenardier knew he was being followed when he entered the grate. He had purposefully sent Valjean out in his place to give the police someone to arrest; to throw them off his own track.

Jean Valjean had been passed from the deadly hands of the mire, to the treacherous hands of Thenardier, to the steel hands of Javert.

Javert too did not recognize Jean Valjean and asked in a quick and calm voice:

"Who are you?"

"I."

"What? I? I asked your name!"

"Jean Valjean."

Javert laid his two powerful hands upon Jean Valjean's shoulders, clamping them like vices as he stared into his eyes until he recognized him. Their faces almost touched. Javert's look was terrible.

"Inspector Javert," said Valjean, "you have got me. Since this morning I have considered myself your prisoner. I did not give you my address to try to escape you. Take me. Only grant me one thing."

Javert rested his fixed eye upon Jean Valjean.

"This man is wounded," said Valjean. "He needs help, now."

"He is dead," said Javert.

Jean Valjean answered:

"No. Not yet."

"You have carried him all the way here from the barricade?" asked Javert in disbelief.

"Yes" answered Valjean. "He lives…I …I don't know where."

Jean Valjean felt in Marius' coat, took out the pocket-book, opened it at the page penciled by Marius, and handed it to Javert.

Javert deciphered the few lines written by Marius, and muttered: "Gillenormand, Calvary Street, No. 6."

Then Javert called out: "Driver?"

Above them on the bank Javert had left a carriage waiting for him in case he apprehended Thenardier.

A moment later Marius was laid upon the back seat, and Javert sat down next to Jean Valjean on the front seat as the carriage rolled off.

It was after nightfall when the carriage arrived at No. 6, Calvary Street.

Jean Valjean and the driver lifted Marius out of the coach as Javert walked with firm steps to the door and called out:

"Somebody here whose name is Gillenormand?"

A doorman opened the door and said: "This is his home. What do you want with him?"

"His son has been to the barricade and got

himself shot. Go and wake his father."

The doorman hurried to the carriage and tried to carry Marius but he was much too small to carry a man.

"Very well," said Javert to Valjean. "Carry him up. I will wait here for you."

Jean Valjean looked at Javert. This seemed very out of place for Javert. Valjean had fled from him before, many times. Why the sudden trust?

Valjean and the doorman carried Marius upstairs and laid him on an old couch while the maid sent for a doctor and then the doorman went to wake Gillenormand.

Gillenormand ran into the room and saw Marius covered in blood and filth.

"Marius! What happened?! Oh, He has got himself killed at the barricade! In hatred of me! It is because of me that he did this! Misery of my life, he is dead!"

He went to a window, opened it wide as if he couldn't breathe with it closed and shouted into the night: "Pierced, stabbed, cut in pieces! WHY?! He knew very well that I was waiting for him, that I had his room ready, that I had his portrait hung at the head of my bed! He knew very well that he had only to come back. He went to the barricades and got himself killed to avenge his father! Why Marius?!"

He turned and fell on his knees by his grandson and looked up just in time to see Marius' eye twitch.

"Marius!" cried the old man. "Marius! My darling

Marius! My child! My dear son! You are opening your eyes, you are looking at me, you are alive, thank God! Thank God!"

Gillenormand fell to the ground having fainted.

Valjean went to close the window and he leaned out over the street to breath in some fresh air. As he did, he looked down.

Jean Valjean was bewildered; there was nobody there.

Javert was gone.

Chapter 8: Doubt

Javert walked with his head down for the first time in his life.

Until that day, Javert had always stood with absolute certainty, with his arms folded across his chest. Now, a change had taken place.

He plunged into the silent streets, taking the shortest route towards the river Seine. He stopped on the bank of the river between the Notre Dame Bridge and the Change Bridge at a point dreaded by mariners. Nothing is more dangerous than this rapid, narrow square. The two bridges, so near each other, make the rapids un-survivable for mariners.

Javert leaned both elbows on the railing. With his chin in his hands, he reflected.

For some hours Javert had ceased to be himself. He was troubled. His brain, always so certain and sure, was now tortured. His crystal clear moral code was now cloudy.

When he had so unexpectedly met Jean Valjean at the sewer outlet he had felt two things at once. He felt like a wolf which had seized his prey a second time, and also like a dog which again found his master.

Valjean had set him free. Now Javert was personally obligated to return the favor. But that would betray justice. Valjean had broken his parole, and should be returned to prison.

What should Javert do now?

What he had already done made him shudder. He, Javert, had let a prisoner go. This went against all the regulations of the police, against the very rules of his life.

A single course of action remained: He must return immediately to Calvary Street and have Jean Valjean arrested. It was clear that this was what he must do, yet he could not.

Something barred the way.

All the truths he had known his entire life crumbled away before this man, Jean Valjean.

Javert remembered the goodness of Valjean when he was Mayor Madeleine, how he had caught him giving money to beggars in Paris, how he had set Javert free, and now had also saved the life of the boy from the barricade. Could there exist a thoughtful thief, a compassionate convict? Javert had to admit that this monster existed.

A convict was his savior! How could he live with it?

Javert now had to deal with something he had never felt before: Doubt.

He now doubted the law. He saw an exception and this horrified him.

Javert looked down into the river. He had been standing in the same spot for nearly an hour.

The darkness was complete. It was the darkest moment of the night. The place where Javert was standing was exactly over the rapids of the Seine river.

Javert leaned forward and looked down further. Everything was black. He heard a frothing sound; but he could not see the river. He took off his hat and laid it on the stone wall at his side. A moment laters, his tall black form was standing on the railing, leaning over the Seine. Suddenly he sprang forward and fell straight into the darkness. There was nothing but a dull splash as his form disappeared under the water.

Chapter 9: Delirium

For several weeks Marius was delirious. He repeated the name of Cosette during entire nights while his grandfather sat by his bedside in despair.

At last, on the 7th of September, four months after the barricade fell, the physician declared Marius out of danger. He was still bed-ridden on account of his shattered shoulder-blade, but he was awake and fully aware of where he was and how lucky he was to be alive.

Gillenormand now called Marius "Sir the Baron." Everything had been forgiven.

As for Marius, he had one fixed thought in his mind: Cosette.

About a week later in the early afternoon, Marius, whose strength had returned, gathered together his courage to try asking his grandfather again for permission to marry. He sat up in bed, rested his clenched hands on the sheets, looked his grandfather in the face, assumed a terrible air, and said:

"I wish to marry."

"I know," said the grandfather. And he burst out laughing.

"How?"

"Her father comes every day to check on you. Who do think has made all these bandages? She's spent months making them every day. She lives in the Homme Street, Number Seven. Ah! You want her! You shall have her. Be happy my dear child and marry."

"Oh Father!" exclaimed Marius.

"Ah! you love me then!" said the old man.

They both became choked up and could not speak.

All the preparations were made for the marriage. The physician said Marius would be healthy enough by February, so the date was set for February 16th.

Jean Valjean made all the preparations. He retrieved all the money he had made as mayor, and presented almost $600,000 as Cosette's dowry.

Marius was now completely confused by Valjean, whom he still knew as Ultimus Fosh. Marius could remember almost nothing that had happened at the barricade, but he thought he remembered seeing Fosh there. But that made no sense. He had memories of Gavroche singing, of Eponine dying, of Enjolras, Coferac, and Comfehr fighting valiantly. Had it all really happened? Were they all really dead? How had he survived?

Marius now felt he owed a debt to two people. There was Thenardier as always, and there was also the unknown man who had carried him away from the barricade and brought him to his grandfather's. Marius persisted in trying to find these two men. Marius still didn't know what really happened at the battle-field of Waterloo. He did not know that Thenardier had never been a savior, but had always been a bandit.

Everywhere Marius looked was a dead end. Madam Thenardier had died in prison. Thenardier and his daughter Azelma had disappeared.

As for the other man, the unknown man who had saved Marius; the search at first had some results, then stopped short. Marius succeeded in finding the carriage which had brought him to his grandfather's house. The driver of the carriage from that night told Marius about being hired by the police, and about nine o'clock in the evening, the grating of the sewer was opened; a man came out, carrying another man on his shoulders. The driver had taken all these men to Calvary Street where they had left the injured man. The man carrying him had never returned while the police officer had paid the driver and walked away.

How did Marius get from the barricade at Chanvrie Road to the sewer outlet? Through the sewer apparently.

Who would do that? Who could do that?

It was this man whom Marius sought.

Marius told Valjean one day about his search for his savior.

"You know what he did, Sir? He must have been like an angel who threw himself into the midst of the combat, snatched me out of it, opened the sewer, dragged me down into it, and carried me through it. He must have made his way for more than four miles, bent over, stooping in the darkness, with me on his back! On coming out of the sewer he was arrested. There is no way to repay that man. I would give the entire six hundred thousand dollars to find that man!"

Jean Valjean kept silent.

Chapter 10: Confession

The 16th of February, 1833, was a blessed day. It was the wedding day of Marius and Cosette. The entire country celebrated, for it happened that the 16th of February that year was also Mardi Gras.

Everyone in the whole city was happy except Jean Valjean. He didn't know what to do.

Cosette had Marius, Marius had Cosette. They had everything, even riches. Valjean had made it happen. Cosette was the most beautiful bride; Marius, the most handsome groom.

But where did Valjean fit in? He was still a convict breaking parole. His life was still a lie. He could not let his ugly past soil Cosette's perfect future. He knew her happiness did not belong to him. He still thought himself unworthy of it.

The day after their wedding, Valjean went to speak to Marius privately.

Marius was so happy to see him he burst out saying:

"Cosette loves you so much! You will live with us, won't you? We've had a room prepared and everything. Sell your old house in Homme street. You will live here with us and the two of you will take walks like you used to at the Luxembourg. You are part of our happiness, do you understand, father? Come now, eat with us."

"Sir," said Jean Valjean, "I have something I must

tell you. I am an old convict."

Marius didn't seem to hear the words, they didn't make any sense to him. He stood there staring at Fosh blankly.

"Sir Pontmercy," said Jean Valjean, "I was nineteen years in prison for robbery. I was a galley-slave. Then I was sentenced for life to parole. At this hour I am in breach of that sentence."

Marius took two steps backward with an expression of unspeakable horror. "But you are Cosette's father."

"No. Sir Baron Pontmercy, I am a peasant who earned his living pruning trees. My name is not Fosh, my name is Jean Valjean. I have no relation to Cosette."

Marius looked at this man. No lie could come out of such calmness.

"I believe you," said Marius.

Jean Valjean inclined his head as if making an oath and continued:

"What am I to Cosette? A passerby. Ten years ago, I did not know that she existed. I love her, it is true. She was an orphan. Without father or mother. She had need of me. That is why I began to love her. Children are so weak, that anybody, even a man like me, may be their protector. I performed that duty with regard to Cosette. Today Cosette leaves my life; our two roads separate. She is now Madam Pontmercy. Her protector is changed. As for the six hundred thousand dollars, it is a trust for her. Your lives go on now as simply the Family Pontmercy. Fosh no longer exists. I am only Jean Valjean."

He stopped and looked Marius in the face.

Marius was stupefied. "Why do you tell me all this? You could have kept your secret. Why tell the truth?"

"Because of honor," said Jean Valjean. "To live, once I stole a loaf of bread; today, to live, I will not even steal a name."

"My grandfather has friends," said Marius. "I will procure your pardon."

"It is useless," answered Jean Valjean. "The police think me dead already. Besides, I don't need a pardon from the government. I need a pardon from only one person, myself."

Valjean added: "There is one thing left-"

"What?"

Jean Valjean hesitated and asked: "Now that you know, do you think that I should stop coming to see Cosette?"

"I think that would be best," answered Marius coldly.

"I… I will obey your wishes. Thank you, Sir," said Jean Valjean.

Valjean turned, and for the last time, walked out the Gillenormand's door.

Chapter 11: Thirty Years in One

Marius was completely unhinged. Who was this man? Cosette's loving father was a convict? He had been to the galleys! Marius now felt repulsed. It had all been lies. Marius was horrified, but somehow, he still felt pity and astonishment.

Why had Valjean revealed himself to Marius? Why ruin his perfect life?

Marius began to review everything he knew of Valjean.

What had really happened at the Jondrette's? Why, when the police arrived had Valjean fled? Now Marius knew the answer. Because he was a fugitive.

Why had Valjean come into the barricade? Marius now remembered; to kill Javert.

Marius remembered seeing Jean Valjean leading Javert,tied-up, to the little side street. Marius recalled hearing the frightful gunshot; the sound of Javert's death.

That was the answer. Jean Valjean had gone to the barricade to avenge himself. Javert must have known his true identity. That is why Valjean had fled at the Thenardiers. That is why Valjean had killed Javert.

Marius now saw Valjean for a demon, a horrific monster. Now only one question remained. How was it possible that Cosette had been filled with so much love when she had been raised by such a man?

Marius began to research Valjean's past when Cosette wasn't around. What he found horrified him.

Any time Cosette asked about her father, Marius made an excuse. Eventually he just told her that her father had left on a long journey. No one knew when he would return, but their lives were happy, and they should live on without him. She was confused, sad, but resigned herself to the oddities of her father.

For months Valjean still took walks every day. Then one day Jean Valjean went down stairs, took a few steps into the street, and instead of continuing out onto the street he sat down upon a stone block. It was the same block where he had seen Gavroche the night the barricade was attacked. Valjean sat there a few minutes, and then went upstairs again. The next day, he did not leave his room. The day after he did not leave his bed.

Soon he stopped eating, only drinking a little water each day.

A week passed, and Jean Valjean had not taken a step out of his bed.

Then one night Jean Valjean had difficulty even raising himself upon his elbow; he felt his own wrist and could not find a pulse; his breathing was short, and even stopped sometimes. He realized that he was weaker than he had been before, so he forced himself to get up and get dressed. The mere effort of putting on his clothes made sweat roll down his forehead.

He opened "the inseparable" and took out Cosette's old clothes.

He spread them out upon his bed.

The bishop's candlesticks were there as well and he moved them to a place of honor on the mantel. He took two wax candles from a drawer, and put them into the candlesticks. Then, although it was still broad daylight during summer, he lit them.

He sat down at his desk and looked in the mirror. He saw himself in this mirror but did not recognize the face. He was eighty years old; before Marius' marriage, people assumed he was only 50; this year had been like thirty for him. What was now upon his forehead was not the wrinkle of age, it was the mysterious mark of death.

He sat there thinking until night came, then with great difficulty he got out pen, ink, and paper.

His hand trembled as he slowly wrote these few lines:

"Cosette, I bless you. I am going to make an explanation to you. Your husband is very good. Always love him well when I am dead. Sir Pontmercy, always love my darling child. Cosette, know that the money I left you is really your own. I once owned a factory making small jewelry. I made a fortune employing hundreds of workers. I saved all that I earned, and now I have given it to you. Have no fear, the money is honorable, it is yours. It was earned in the city of-

Here he stopped, the pen fell from his fingers, he let out a despairing sob and cried out:

"Oh! It is all over. I shall never see her again. Oh!

What I'd give to hear her voice, to touch her dress, to look at her, the angel! Then I could die. It is nothing to die, but it is dreadful to die without seeing her. She would smile upon me, she would say a kind word to me. No, it is over, forever. Here I am, all alone. My God! My God! I shall never see her again."

At this moment there was a knock at his door.

Chapter 12: Thenard

Hearing a knock at his door, Marius opened it to see a doorman with a letter.

"The writer of this letter waits for you below sir," said the doorman as he handed over the letter.

Marius looked at the letter. It seemed very familiar. It was written on coarse paper, was poorly folded, and it stunk of tobacco. Marius remembered the letters he had found from Thenardier disguised as Jondrette years ago.

Marius broke the seal and read-

"Sir Barón,-

I am in possession of a secret conserning an individual you know well. I dezire the honor of being yuseful to you.

I await you below.-

With respect.

-THENARD."

Marius had a feeling of happiness. He could finally repay his father's debt, and maybe his other debt as well. Maybe Thenardier's secret was the identity of the man who had saved his life! Marius opened one of his desk drawers, took out some cash bills, put them in his pockets, and welcomed Thenardier into his office.

"Sir the Baron. I have a secret to sell you."

"Which concerns me?"

"Somewhat."

"What is this secret?"

"I'll start for free, but after that you must pay," said Thenardier.

"Go on."

"Sir Baron, you have in your house a robber and an assassin. This man has glided into your confidence, and almost into your family, under a false name. I am going to tell you his true name."

"I am listening."

"His name is Jean Valjean."

"I know it."

"I am going to tell you, also for nothing, who he is."

"Say on."

"He is an old convict."

"I know that too."

Thenardier now looked flustered. How could Marius know these things, he wondered.

"The secret I have concerns the fortune of your wife. It is an extraordinary secret. It is for sale. I offer it to you for twenty thousand dollars."

"I know the secret as well as the others," said Marius.

"Sir Baron, just offer me then, say, ten thousand dollars, and I will go on."

"You have nothing new to tell me – I know all this."

"Fine. Just give me twenty dollars."

Marius looked at him steadily: "I know your

extraordinary secret; just as I knew Jean Valjean's name: just as I know your name."

"My name? That is not difficult, Sir Baron. I have told it to you and I wrote it in the letter. My name is Thenard."

"Thenard-ier," said Marius. "You used to own an inn at Montfermeil. You are a scoundrel and a thief and for your one good deed I pay you now once and for all!

Marius, taking a bank-note from his pocket, threw it in Thenardier's face.

"Five hundred dollars!" exclaimed Thenardier. "Thank you Sir Baron!"

"Thenardier, I have told you your name. Do you want me to tell you the secret too? Jean Valjean, as you have said, is an assassin and a robber. A robber, because he robbed a rich manufacturer, Mayor Madeleine, whose ruin he caused. Valjean is also an assassin, because he assassinated the police-officer, Javert."

"I don't understand Sir Baron," said Thenardier.

"Listen. Back in 1822, a man named M. Madeleine made a fortune for himself and for an entire city. I have spent great time and funds finding this information out. This mayor founded hospitals, opened schools, visited the sick, supported widows, adopted orphans; he was, as it were, the guardian of the country. A liberated convict informed against him and had him arrested, and took his entire fortune, six hundred thousand dollars. This convict who robbed

M. Madeleine is Jean Valjean. As to the other act, you have just as little to tell me. Jean Valjean killed the police officer Javert; He shot him the night the barricade fell. I know this because I was there, I saw it happen."

Thenardier sat in a stupor.

"Sir Baron, you are mistaken. Jean Valjean never robbed Mayor Madeleine, and he never killed Javert."

"How is that?"

"The first is this: he did not rob Mayor Madeleine, since Jean Valjean himself was Mayor Madeleine. And he did not assassinate Javert, since Javert killed himself."

"What do you mean?"

"Javert committed suicide."

"Prove it! prove it!" cried Marius, beside himself.

Thenardier took out two newspapers. The oldest was from a newspaper which detailed the confession of Mayor Madeleine to being the convict Jean Valjean. He had done it in a courtroom in Arras. The other newspaper verified the suicide of Javert, adding that Javert had told a fellow officer that he had only escaped the barricades because of the kindness of an insurgent who could have killed him, but had fired into the air instead.

Marius read both papers, astonished. Here was unquestionable proof. Marius could not doubt as he cried out with joy:

"All that fortune is really his own! He is Mayor Madeleine, the savior of a whole region! He is Jean

Valjean, the savior of Javert! He is a hero! He is a saint!"

"He is not a saint, and he is not a hero," said Thenardier. "He is an assassin and a robber. Jean Valjean did not rob Madeleine, but he is a robber. He did not kill Javert, but he is a murderer. Sir Baron, on the 6th of June, 1832, about a year ago, the day after the attempted revolution, I was in the sewer near the river Seine. I came across a man carrying a corpse on his back. The man was an old convict, an assassin if ever there was one. This convict was going to throw his corpse into the river. It was odd that he still had the body. He had just passed through a horrible mire in which he easily could have left the body. His efforts must have been terrible; I do not understand how he came out of it alive."

Marius' chair drew nearer. Thenardier took advantage of it to draw a long breath. He continued:

"Sir Baron, this man said to me: I must get out, you have the key, give it to me.' This convict was a man of terrible strength. There was no refusing him. I stalled in order to give myself some time. I examined the dead man and managed to tear off, without the assassin noticing, a piece of the dead man's coat; a piece of evidence, so I could later help the police identify the victim and the criminal. I then let the convict out with the corpse on his back, shut the grating again and I escaped. The assassin, the convict, was Jean Valjean. I'd recognize him anywhere."

Thenardier finished by drawing from his pocket a

strip of ragged black cloth, covered with dark stains.

Marius was pale, hardly breathing, his eye fixed upon the black cloth. He stumbled backward, never taking his eye off the cloth, and groped behind him for a key on the desk.

He found the key and turned and opened the closet.

"The dead man was me, and here is the coat!" cried Marius, as he threw an old black coat covered with blood onto the carpet.

Then, snatching the fragment from Thenardier's hands, he bent down over the coat, and put the piece in its place. The edges fit exactly.

Thenardier was petrified.

Marius bellowed at Thenardier as he began shoving him toward the door.

"You are a wretch! You are a liar, a slanderer, a scoundrel. You came to accuse this man? It is you who are a robber! You who are an assassin! Now get out! I should have you arrested but Waterloo protects you."

"Waterloo?" muttered Thenardier, pocketing the five hundred dollars.

"Yes. Here, take three thousand dollars more. Take it all and tomorrow morning start for America. I will see to your departure, bandit. Go and get hung someplace else!"

"Sir Baron," answered Thenardier, bowing to the ground, "my eternal gratitude."

Thenardier left without understanding anything

that had happened. He was just happy with the fortune he had just made. It happened that two days later he did leave for America and remained the same man he had been in Europe; still a bandit, still a thief.

As soon as Thenardier was out of his house, Marius ran to the garden where Cosette was walking:

"Cosette! Cosette!" cried he. "Come! Come quick! Let us go. It was he who saved my life! Let us not lose a minute!"

Marius was in a fog which was quickly clearing. He began to see Valjean for what he was, an angel of virtue, humble in his greatness. The convict now took on the image of Christ.

Marius ran to the carriage and helped Cosette in while telling the driver, "Homme Street, Number 7. Hurry!"

"Oh! what happiness!" said Cosette. "Homme Street! Is father back from his journey?"

"Your father! It was he went to the barricade to save me. He not only saved me, but he saved others; he saved Javert. He carried me on his back in that frightful sewer. Oh! How ungrateful I have been. He carried me through a terrible mire, almost drowning himself. We are going to bring him back to live with us whether he wants to or not. He shall never leave us again. Cosette, it all makes sense now. Do you understand?"

Cosette did not understand a word.

CHAPTER 13: COMING HOME

At the knock which he heard at his door, Jean Valjean turned his head.

"Come in," he said feebly.

The door opened. Cosette and Marius rushed in.

"Cosette!" said Jean Valjean. He rose in his chair, his arms stretched out, trembling, with immense joy in his eyes.

"Father!" she said, running to embrace him.

"Is it you, Cosette? You are here? You forgive me then!" He stammered. "How foolish I was! I thought I should never see you again. I was saying to myself just now "It is over." How silly of me to doubt God. God knew I needed my angel, now my angel comes. I see my Cosette again!"

Cosette continued her caresses as she asked: "Where have you been? Why were you away so long?"

Marius broke in: "Cosette, your father has saved my life, brought us together, and then willingly sacrificed himself. He gave up his own happiness thinking that he had to for our happiness to be complete. Cosette, that man is an angel!"

"Hush! hush!" said Jean Valjean in a whisper. "Why tell all that?"

"But you!" exclaimed Marius, "Why have you not told it? It is your fault, too. You save people's lives, and you hide it from them! Tomorrow you are moving in with us. For good!"

"Tomorrow," said Jean Valjean, "I shall not be here, but I shall not be at your house either."

"What do you mean?" replied Marius. "You shall never leave us again. We will not let you go."

Cosette took both the old man's hands in her own.

"My God!" she said, "your hands are like ice. Are you sick? Are you suffering?"

"No," answered Jean Valjean. "I am very well. Only…"

He stopped.

"Only what?" she asked.

"I am dying."

Cosette and Marius shuddered.

"Dying!" exclaimed Marius.

"Yes, but that is nothing," said Jean Valjean.

Cosette uttered a piercing cry:

"Father! My father! You shall live. I will have you live, do you hear?"

Jean Valjean raised his head towards her with love.

"Oh, yes, forbid me to die. Who knows? I shall obey perhaps. I was just dying when you came. You stopped me."

"Father, you cannot die," cried Cosette.

"It is nothing to die; it is frightful not to live." He answered.

Suddenly Valjean arose. These returns of strength are sometimes a sign of the death-struggle. He walked with a firm step to the wall, took down a little copper crucifix which hung there and laid it on the table:

"Behold the great martyr."

Then his breast sank in, his head wavered as if the dizziness of the tomb seized him, and he rested his hands upon his knees.

"Father, are you in pain?" asked Marius.

"Do you want a priest?" asked Cosette.

"I have one," answered Jean Valjean.

And, with his finger, he seemed to designate a point above his head, where he seemed to see the Bishop, coming to take him to heaven.

With each moment Jean Valjean grew weaker. His face grew pale and at the same time he smiled. He began to speak to them in a voice so faint it seemed to come from afar.

"Cosette, on the desk you will find my letter. To you I leave the two candlesticks which are on the mantel. They are made of silver; but to me they are gold. I do not know whether he who gave them to me is satisfied with me in heaven. I have done what I could. I hope I have pleased him. Sir Pontmercy, I offer my last confessions. I must confess to you that I have not always loved you; I ask your pardon. Cosette, do you see your little dress, there on the bed? Do you recognize it? It was only ten years ago. How time passes! Do you remember Montfermeil? You were in the woods. You were very frightened. Do you remember when I took the handle of the water-bucket? That time I touched your poor little hand. It was so cold! And the great doll! Do you remember? You called her Catherine. How you made me laugh sometimes, my sweet angel! You have forgotten it. Those are things of the past. Those Thenardiers were wicked. We must forgive them. Cosette, the time has come to tell of your mother. Her name was Fantine. Remember that name: Fantine. Fall on your knees whenever you pronounce it. She suffered much and she loved much. God took her home and gave you to me. He is on high, he sees us all, and he knows what he does in the midst of his great stars."

Valjean looked at them both intently: "Love each other dearly always. There is scarcely anything else in the world but that: to love one another. My children, I had some more things to say, but it makes no difference. I see a light. Come nearer. I die happy. Let me put my hands upon your dear beloved heads."

Cosette and Marius fell on their knees, overwhelmed, choked with tears, each grasping one of Jean Valjean's hands. His hands moved no more.

The light from the candlesticks fell upon him. His white face looked up towards heaven as he let Cosette and Marius cover his hands with kisses; he was gone.

EPILOGUE

In a poor cemetery, in a deserted corner, beneath a great yew tree, there is a stone. This stone has been weathered by time and now appears entirely blank. No name can be read there.

Many years ago, a hand wrote upon it in pencil these four lines which have become faded under the rain and the dust, and which are probably now gone:

He sleeps, although his fate was very strange
He lived for his angel, and died when she was gone
His death came to pass simply
As the night comes when the day is gone.

THE END

Made in the USA
Columbia, SC
24 August 2018